HOW KIRSTY GETS HER KICKS

JENNIFER LEE **THOMSON**

How Kirsty Gets Her Kicks

SH OTGUN
H O NEY

Published by Shotgun Honey, an imprint of Down & Out Books

Shotgun Honey
PO Box 75272
Charleston, WV 25375
www.ShotgunHoney.com

Down & Out Books
3959 Van Dyke Rd, Ste. 265
Lutz, FL 33558
www.DownAndOutBooks.com

Cover Design by Bad Fido.

First Printing 2019

ISBN-10: 1-64396-005-9
ISBN-13: 978-1-64396-005-0

For Benjy.
The happiest person I've
ever had the privilege of knowing.

HOW KIRSTY
GETS HER KICKS

One

AS THE RANCID STENCH of the pug ugly bastard, who'd groped her for the last time snaked up Kirsty's nostrils, making them twitch like a thoroughbred at Ayr racecourse, she threw back her fiery red hair.

"Fuck this," she said, aiming a knee-high kick a Can-can dancer would have been proud of squarely in his groin.

The resounding squelch as her stiletto clad foot connected with his balls, gave her as much satisfaction as the whimper that erupted from his throat as he fell, gasping for breath, cradling himself.

As she stood over him, a wicked smile playing on her lips, he hissed through clenched teeth. "You fucking bitch."

"Too bloody right I am."

She spoke in the same singsong voice she used to extract cash from punters who wouldn't pay and kicked him again, this time full force in the head. Blood oozed out of his forehead where her stiletto went in and silenced his ugly mouth. With a sense of triumph, she noticed there was a hole in his head like he'd been gored by a bull. *Better watch his brains don't dribble out.*

She heard a suction noise as she pulled the heel clear. The sound reminded her of the noise a vacuum cleaner makes when a sock becomes trapped in the air stream and you pull it free without switching it off first.

"Kirsty, what did you do?"

Her 100 watt smile dimmed when she heard the frightened wee voice of barman, Jamie, the one guy in this hellhole who didn't try to cop a feel. She thought he'd gone home.

Flicking away a stray strand of hair that dared to land on her face, she lowered her green eyes; they shone like headlights ruining her attempt to appear demure. In these situations being dressed in a figure hugging PVC skirt and blouse that showcased her curves didn't help, not when you were going for the vulnerability card.

"I think he tripped," she said, wiping her stiletto on the floor. It left a trail of blood and gunge that might have been brain matter – if the bastard had actually had a brain. Glancing down, she was happy to see that most of the blood was off her shoe and the thing wasn't ruined; those shoes were expensive.

Jamie shook his blonde head and his brow furrowed, making him appear much older than the kid he was. He leaned in so close he could have been about to kiss her, and said in a hushed voice, "You don't know who that is, do you?"

She met his concern with a heavy stare and he shrunk back. "Nah and I don't bloody care either."

"It's one of Jimmy McPhee's enforcers." He spoke with a reverence the knuckle draggers didn't deserve. But then everyone in Glasgow spoke that way about those who scared them shitless.

Kirsty had hung round here long enough to know that

In gangland speak, enforcer was the title of a thug who went around cracking skulls and kneecaps with hammers and baseball bats, once they'd stubbed out their lit cigarettes on your eyes and thrown boiling water in your face; and that was for a warm up if they liked you. Once you'd got acquainted, then they turned real nasty. Kirsty knew what kind of man owned the club, but beggars couldn't be choosers; she needed this job.

Kirsty batted her long eyelashes, giving her the wide Bambi eyes men were such suckers for, then said loud enough for her victim to hear, "I don't fucking care. He was touching me up. Next guy does that gets *it* bitten off."

Jamie didn't need to ask what it meant. He covered his groin area with his hands and stepped further back. He could have been a footballer facing the might of a Brazilian free kick.

A twisted grin spread across Kirsty's face. Men thought women were weak, but a well-aimed kick between the legs sure leveled the playing field.

"Nah, you're okay," she said with a saucy wink, but he wasn't reassured. Maybe because he'd just witnessed her kicking the crap out of a growler more used to dishing it out than being on the receiving end.

Jamie pulled a stool out and slunk down in it, the color washed out of his face as if he was a painting that'd been left out in the rain. Meanwhile, the groping bastard lay howling on the floor, curled up, a wee boy wanting his mammy; the last woman, Kirsty reckoned had willingly let him anywhere near her business end.

"What the hell are we going to do now?" Jamie asked, making eye contact and then breaking it off because he was scared of what he saw in her eyes.

"Well, I could hit him again."

She didn't mean it. Messing up one shoe was bad enough without ruining another. They were too expensive. Besides, if she kicked him with her other leg it was liable to fly off. Prosthetic limbs tended to do that, unless you were Heather Mills and could afford the best.

"Okay, okay, Jamie, don't get your knickers in a twist. I'm only joking."

What the hell was she going to do? Concentration lined her forehead and she didn't like that because it gave her frown lines.

The way she saw it there were two options. She could hang around and be tortured by some sicko with a blow-torch and a small cock who'd enjoy passing her round his pals before they cut off her tits and fed them to their steroid boosted pit bulls, or she could get the fuck out of here with some spending money.

She moistened her lips with her tongue. "Well, I was planning on running off with the takings."

Jamie shivered and slowly lowered his head into his hands and started muttering "fuck, fuck, fuck," as he rocked about in the stool. He said something about "crazy bitch," and she grinned. Now he got her.

After a few minutes of mumbling to himself, he lifted his head and took in the view before his eyes finally rested on her collarbone in a barely concealed attempt to hide the fact he'd been staring at her boobs. Most men did that; kids wanting to put their paws in the sweetie jar. From now on, if any man tried getting handy a slap was the least of their worries, now the precedent had been set.

"The boss will kill me if you nick the cash," he said.

The boss he was referring to was Jimmy McPhee who owned the joint; a mean bastard with an eye for pretty girls – ones not old enough to leave school. Jimmy was into all sorts: drug dealing, extortion, money lending and laundering and prostitution. He was an expert in creative persuasion, or as most people would call it, torture.

Kirsty knew this, but she made sure that whilst working in his club it was a case of see no evil, hear no evil. Sure, she hated this seedy little shit-hole, but the tips were good and who else would employ her when she was the wrong side of thirty with a temper to match her hair and one leg? The punters enjoyed their wee jousts. A few even wanted to marry her.

Kirsty shrugged. "I could always give you a doing as well. That would solve the problem." She paused, and then added with a devilish grin, "No enough to kill you mind."

"Ha fucking ha," said Jamie. Kirsty gave him a sideways glance. He moved back in his stool, held up his hand in a placatory fashion and said, "Sorry."

She giggled; a child's giggle. It sounded strange coming from her lips. "Nothing to be sorry for, mister. I'm the one who's screwed up your night. I thought it was just me and shit for brains over there." She cocked a finger at the limp, dirty bastard bleeding onto the floor. Bar manager Angie would be pleased.

Kirsty's left leg was starting to itch and she took it off so she could give the stump a scratch. As she did, she could feel Jamie's gaze upon her. He'd stopped fixating on her boobs she knew resembled two bobbling apples in the gypsy blouse she wore to get more tips. Some dumb fucks assumed they were part of the complimentary buffet and tried to touch them, but she always put them in their place – usually running to the bog every two minutes because of the laxatives she put in their drinks.

Jamie was gaping at the leg, mesmerized by the thing. "It's fake." He eyed the leg as if she'd just whipped off her top and started sucking her own nipples.

"No shit, Sherlock. What gave the game away?"

If he heard the sarcasm in her voice, he ignored it as he wittered on about what her leg as if he was telling his pals about a new video game release. "Wow. You took out one of McPhee's boys with one bloody leg. Awesome. You're like that bird in the Robert Rodriguez zombie movie. Rose McGowan played her."

In all the excitement, his fear dissolved, an Alka-Seltzer in water. She could handle the wide-eyed admiration. But then he went and ruined it all by asking her the question she hated more than Glaswegian drunks at chucking out time.

"How did you lose your leg?"

His admiration evaporated, replaced by something that made her want to hit him repeatedly about the skull with her prosthetic. Pity. *Shit, as if things weren't bad enough. Now John Boy Walton felt sorry for her.*

Her lips went as tight as the zip on a bulging purse. She wasn't going to tell him. Let him bloody guess.

One glimpse at his disappointed wee face and she relented. What the hell? Might as well get the pity pish out the way, so they could deal with the more pressing stuff, like how the hell to get out of here without having her false leg rammed up her backside by one of McPhee's cronies. And that was the least they would do to her. She was cursed with a vivid imagination and could picture all manner of sick things those psychos would inflict on her.

Through the tiny slit in her mouth she spoke. "Okay, I'll tell you what happened, but afterwards you'd better stop eye-balling me as if I'm a poor little cripple girl. I fuckin' hate that. Okay?"

Jamie's gaze fell on his shoes, moved along the floor, resting anywhere but on her. "You don't have to tell me."

He was trying to act as if he didn't care. But, there was a spark in his eyes and he'd become a kid on Christmas Eve, poking and prodding away at the biggest, brightest, shiniest present.

She raised her eyebrows. "You really want to know, huh?"

He met her gaze and nodded.

Her voice was a dull monotone when she spoke. Instead of talking about her own life she could have been one of those directory enquiries call center drones. That's what happened when you told a story so often it was like you were talking about someone else, or a movie you'd seen. "I was in a car crash when I was eight. Both my parents died, along with my wee brother Joe. They were forced to cut off my leg to free me. End of story."

Jamie's face darkened. "That's terrible." He went back to examining his shoes, the bar, looking anywhere to avoid her gaze. There was something unmistakable in his expression too.

"Is that fucking sadness I see in your eyes?" The glare she gave him could have scorched the earth, but he didn't wilt under it which made him unique. Men had been reduced to stuttering eejits by that glare.

She threw back her head and gave a throaty laugh. The static electricity caused by the movement caused sparks to fly from the bonfire that was her hair. Poor sod Jamie jumped ten feet in the air.

She winked at him and he relaxed. "Only messing with you."

His mouth relaxed. He was acting as if he'd known all along. He blinked. "Right."

"What happened was I spotted my boyfriend with his hand up the skirt of another girl as I went by on the train. I stuck my leg out to kick him up the arse. The train started moving at the time and splat. My leg came off at the knee."

She made a severing motion with her hand and suppressed a giggle when his face turned the color of putty.

Jamie made a funny gagging noise and put his hand over his mouth as if about to puke, but he didn't.

'So, what's the truth?" His gaze was clear and direct.

"Whatever you want to believe," she told him. Behind all her lies was a slither of truth. The truth was whatever folk wanted it to be, or whatever suited her at the time. "Now for the cash," she said.

"I thought you were kidding." His life was no doubt flashing before him as he envisioned life on the run from those who carried other folk's knuckle bones as knuckle dusters. "If we take the cash they'll come after us."

"You can cut out this "we," she snorted. "I'm the one who's taking the money. You happened to be here. Why are you here anyway? It's closing time. Don't you have a home to go to student boy, where a nice lassie's waiting for you with a pot noodle and some microchips?"

He shrugged. "I stayed back to tidy up. Nobody's waiting at home for me." Then he gave her a weary eyeball and said, "Maybe I should go home."

Kirsty frowned. The guy could not be serious. "Nah, you can't. How do you think McPhee will see it when he finds Zombieland over there, dead..." she nodded towards the octopus, "and his cash and us gone?"

Jamie stood there, glaikit as ever. Christ, she was going to have to spell it out for the sap. He was so innocent he was Bambi. "He'll think you were in on it."

He winced. "He's not dead. He can't be."

Kirsty pursed her lips. She hated to rain on his parade, but... "Of course he is, or if he isn't he soon will be. He's got a great bloody hole in his head. It's not like he's had keyhole surgery. No one can survive a stiletto heel to the brain. Trust me."

Jamie got off his stool and peered at the prone figure on the carpet. There was no more moaning, no movement at all. Jamie put his head in his hands in an all too familiar pose. "Shit. He is dead."

He sank back into his bar stool and repeatedly thumped his head off the bar.

She left him to it for a moment and marched over. "Jamie," she said sharply, "stop it. It aint helping mister."

He didn't stop, so she grabbed him by the hair and pulled him towards her until his goggle eyes were level with her boobs. Now she'd got his attention, it was time to shake him out of his stupor. "Jamie, we have to get going."

"Eh?" He hadn't taken his eyes off her breasts and she couldn't blame him. They were mighty fine specimens.

"We have to get the cash."

"Aw right," he said, not shifting his gaze.

That's when she lifted his head up with her two hands and smacked it hard against the counter. It made a resounding thump that pleased her.

He yelped in surprise. "What did you do that for?"

He stood with fists clenched as if he was gonna hit her. But if she knew one thing in life it was if a man was going to hit you he'd just do it, not telegraph it.

Standing close to his ear she said, "Now you've done being sorry for yourself, it's time to shift your backside. Not unless you want to be swimming with the fishes, chopped up in wee bits."

Her wee pep talk worked and he was on his feet and following her to the back of the club where the office was. The pervy bastard she'd lamped was in her way and she kicked him so hard his body bounced along the carpet. No sign of life. He was as chatty as anyone would be who'd had a stiletto embedded in their skull.

Peering down at her victim, she fought the temptation to see how many fingers she could get inside the hole. When would she ever get the chance to do that again? Not wanting to ruin her expensive manicure, she quickly dismissed the idea.

When they got to the office, she gave the door a shove. It wouldn't budge.

"Bugger," she scowled. "The lock's so gammy that even when Jimmy thinks it's locked you can usually open it with a shove."

Jamie sounded relieved. "Well that's it. You can't get in so you can't get the cash." He turned to walk away. Way too fast for her liking.

She shot him a scornful look and he shrunk back. "Jamie, don't be so defeatist." Licking her lips, she held out her hand. "Credit card."

That puzzled him. "What?"

"I need your credit card to get this door open."

"Don't have one."

But she wasn't going to be fooled. "You're a student having to work in a shitty little place. Of course you've got a credit card. You'll be living off the thing."

He put his hand in his front pocket and produced a MasterCard in the name Jamie Stewart. Grudgingly, he extended his hand. She snatched the card and grabbed him by his collar and kissed him hard on the lips. His face turned the color of strawberries.

"Ta."

Nimbly she slid the card into the vertical crack between the doorframe and the doorjamb, then tilted it. With a bit of maneuvering the door was open in less than a minute.

Jamie sighed. All along, he'd been hoping she'd fail. *He was no fun that one.*

"Step away from the door."

The voice that came when the door opened made them both jump. It was Jimmy McPhee's.

Two

JAMIE WAS ALMOST at the exit when Kirsty called him back. There was a nervous smile on her lips. Although she'd never admit it, she'd thought for a sinking nanosecond that McPhee was there, but unlike Jamie she'd stood her ground.

What was the point in running: she wasn't going to get anywhere very fast in these heels. If she'd known this morning that she'd been going on the run she would have brought more practical shoes.

"It's okay, Jamie. Just one of those motion activated things." Then she added as much for her own benefit as for his, "As if that's going to fool anyone."

A sheepish Jamie reappeared. His jeans wore the telltale wet patch at the groin. *Poor kid must have pissed himself.* Not that she was going to mention it. She'd fucked up his life enough without making a big deal out of it.

"Where's the money?" He did his best to sound nonchalant.

"There's a safe. Behind one of the pictures on the wall."

McPhee's office was much naffer than she remembered. There was a huge chair behind a mahogany desk that would have cost a bundle, but it resembled something you'd find in a skip because it was clad in a leopard skin cover; the only thing missing was the fluffy dice. The walls were a mixture of wooden paneling and what appeared to be the kind of leather upholstery you'd expect to find in a car. A lone light bulb swung from the ceiling, maybe to make McPhee and his cronies feel at home because it'd remind them of getting grilled by the cops.

The light bulb went on in Jamie's head and his dumb expression was gone. "How do you know where the safe is?" he asked.

She ignored the question and lifted a picture of McPhee standing next to Glen Michael, of Glen Michael's Cavalcade fame, frowning when she realized there was nothing behind the picture but dust. She began inspecting the other pictures along the walls. Some were of McPhee with local sporting heroes, mainly boxers and two bit beauty queens who at best would snag an Old Firm player and at worst someone who played for Motherwell.

Jamie pointed towards a picture of the Mona Lisa with enormous breasts. "It might be behind this one." He lifted the picture up and flashed a triumphant smile when it revealed the hidden safe. Kirsty giggled. Talk about a clichéd place to keep your stash. McPhee was pretty dumb.

Their smiles faded when Jamie turned the lock in the safe and it sprung open without even having to enter a combination. It was empty. A useless dummy safe. McPhee wasn't as dumb as he appeared.

Kirsty dropped to the floor. "Shit," she wailed, "I should have known it was too fucking easy. What do I do now?" She could feel worry lines appearing where they'd no right to be.

She needed a quick getaway, but that wasn't going to happen now. If one of McPhee's cronies walked in the door they'd be toast.

Jamie replaced the picture. "Well, unless we can get Peter Petrelli to bring the man you battered back to life so he can tell us where the safe is and the Haitian to wipe his memory, we can either do one of two things." He paused as if waiting for the imaginary drum roll to end. She would have been interested if she knew what the hell he was talking about. "*Heroes*," he said. When she looked at him blankly, he said: "It's a TV show."

She nudged him with his arm, because if she battered him to death with her fake leg he wouldn't be able to say what was on his mind. "Do you need to be such a bloody geek?" she said rolling her eyes. "I haven't got time for this."

Jamie cleared his throat. "The way I see it we can get the hell out of here without the money, or look for another safe. McPhee's not daft. He must have a dummy safe for a reason – to hide the fact there's a real one." He waved his arms around the room. "Now where could that be?"

Kirsty relaxed. "You're smarter than you look." She stopped to think for a minute. "People expect a safe to be on the wall, but what if it's inside a piece of furniture, or on the floor somewhere?"

Ten minutes later, the office looked like it'd been hit by a tornado. Drawers were smashed open, chairs were thrown about, pictures torn from the wall and discarded on the floor. The bin was still spinning from all the times it'd been kicked in frustration.

There was one place they hadn't checked. Next to the desk was a novelty fridge in the shape of a can of *Budweiser*. They looked at each other. Kirsty was first to the fridge. She popped up the lid and started lifting out cans of McEwen's

Export, resisting the urge to take a slug. This wasn't the time to get pie eyed. She needed to stay focused.

Once the fridge was empty she started feeling around the inside trying to find any hint this was more than a simple way of keeping the cold beers coming.

Feeling along the bottom, she shrieked with delight. Underneath the cans there was a false bottom. She pulled and hauled at the plastic, tried to get her fingernails underneath it, but couldn't get the bottom to budge.

"Let me try," said Jamie, nudging her aside. And for once she let him. There was a feverish excitement in his words, as if he knew what he was doing. He stuck his head right in the fridge and muttered away to himself. Less than 30 seconds later, he jumped up and yelled, "Got it."

Kirsty followed his gaze. There was a safe half wedged in the can and the floor. Unlike the decoy one they'd found this one was shut. They needed the combination. Pronto.

Three

HER GAZE MOVED from the safe to Jamie and back again to the safe. She took a deep breath that went all the way down to her soles.

She gazed at the safe, over at Jamie and then back again as if that would give her some answers. "Any ideas, Sherlock?" she finally said.

The safe was a small steel box with an electronic combination lock instead of the dial she'd been expecting. There was also a keyhole, presumably for a key to be used if the person forgot the combination. At least she hoped you didn't need the two at once. Getting the combination would be tricky enough without having to find a key as well.

Jamie shook his head. "The combination could be anything."

Kirsty tutted. "Anything. Well, that's a big help." He gave her that choir boy look to remind her yet again that she was the one who'd corrupted him.

Jamie's baby blues dimmed. "How about a memorable

date? His birthday? The day he got married? Something to do with football?" He paused and raised his eyes to the ceiling, as if he'd get the answer there. "The day his kids were born. I dunno."

Kirsty shook her head. "I don't think he's the kind of guy to use his own birthday or wedding day, do you? Especially when from what I've heard he hates his wife's guts and once tried to get her killed, or maybe it was her who put a price on his head." In McPhee's world, it was hard to separate the bullshit from the lies. "As for kids, don't think he's got any. Story goes that old Jimmy's firing blanks."

Not that anyone dare say that to his face. Nobody wanted a beer glass shoved in their face.

Jamie's whole body shook as he laughed. "That'll go down well in the circles he moves in."

Kirsty wasn't laughing. There was a gruesome image in her mind she needed to share. "From what I hear, the last person who joked about that ended up eating his own cock."

"What?" said Jamie, moving one hand down his trousers to make sure his was still there. "How did they get him to do that?"

"Jimmy cut it off whilst he was still alive and then shoved it in the bloke's mouth, at least that's how the story goes. Poor bastard choked to death on it." Kirsty spoke matter-of-factly. She'd heard the story a number of times and it still sickened her, but no way was she letting her distaste show. Not to choirboy Jamie. Let him keep thinking she was an unfeeling psycho bitch from hell. Men who feared her tended to do her bidding.

"The way you talk it's as if this is normal in your world," said Jamie.

"Na, you get used to hearing about that stuff. Think of the worst thing you've ever heard and times it by ten and that gives you some idea of what goes on."

"Jesus, I don't want any part of that kind of world," said Jamie, in his holier than now tone.

His attitude made Kirsty want to throttle him. Was he suggesting she choose this life?

He'll learn that sometimes you take a wrong turning in life and before you know it, there's no way back and you're completely fucked.

Kirsty frowned. "Neither did I, but it kind of creeps up on you. I was the same as you once. I went to college and wanted to make something of myself. Then life came and knocked me on my backside and before I knew it I'm working in this flea pit."

"Couldn't you have got out? Made something of yourself?"

He made it sound so easy.

"Quit the psychoanalysis." Her tone was sharp. For a moment, she eyed him the way a snake eyes its prey.

Taking a gulp of air, she let it all out until her anger subsided. What did he know? Probably came from a good family from somewhere posh like Bearsden and had no concept of life in the real world, where nobody gave a shit about anyone but themselves. But, right now she needed his help.

"We need to figure out what this combination is," she said. "Maybe he's written it down somewhere? The McPhee's of this world aren't renowned for their brains. The reason they're loaded is they do stuff that no decent person would ever consider doing to another human being."

A smile twitched across Jamie's face. "And you told me to quit the psychoanalysis? You're pretty good at it yourself."

She ignored him and began meticulously searching the office for scraps of paper, diaries, books, notepads, business cards, and takeaway menus - anything he could have written the numbers on.

18

Her efforts produced precisely zilch.

She slumped down on McPhee's movie director chair, resigned to the fact she was going to have to beast a hasty retreat without the cash.

She'd dragged herself out of the chair and was heading for the door, when she saw it: the picture of a page 3 girl torn out of a newspaper and blue tacked to the outside of his desk drawer. Classy. The girl was wearing nothing but a g-string and a too wide smile; she was probably bored out her brain and deciding whether to have beans on toast or pizza for dinner.

What caught Kirsty's eye was her vital statistics, tastefully detailed in the short blurb that accompanied the picture: "42-24-34." The figures were underlined with a red felt tip pen. For a crime boss Jimmy McPhee was pretty dumb.

Triumphantly she jumped up in the air. "Jamie, I've got it."

He seemed under-whelmed and she couldn't work out why. She needed money to get away and the sooner she was out of his hair the better, surely? Anyway she didn't have time for his sulking; there was a safe load of lovely money calling her.

She entered the numbers and the safe opened with a satisfying click. Kirsty didn't have to put her hand inside to find the cash. There were rolls of used twenties spilling out, all tied tightly in bundles with elastic bands. There were at least twenty bundles.

She tore off an elastic band and started counting the cash as Jamie stood there wide eyed. There were twenty five twenties. Five grand in just one bundle. A huge smile swept across her face.

"So fucking easy. This is so fucking easy." She sang in the style of a football chant, throwing bundles of notes at Jamie.

He leapt after them like a puppy chasing a ball, his smile so big it must have hurt.

Kirsty stopped singing. There was the unmistakable shape of a gun wrapped in a piece of cloth at the far side of the safe. Gently, she lifted up the cloth; the last thing she wanted to do was to shoot herself in the face. Wrapped alongside it were some bullets. She counted six of them.

Using the cloth she lifted up the revolver. Close up, she could see it was loaded. It was heavy and she liked the way it felt as she dropped it into the pocket of her hoodie. No wonder men with guns acted like they had two cocks. A gun gave you power: the power to decide whether someone should live or die.

She picked up the bullets. She got the sense she'd need them.

At that very moment, excitement burrowed inside her. She wanted the chance to use the weapon, to feel the reassuring weight in her hand. To know that someone was at her mercy.

The feeling was intoxicating, but sickening at the same time. Was she turning into one of the men she despised?

Jamie was too busy counting the money to notice what she was doing, which was just as well: if he caught sight of it, he'd probably have pissed his pants, again.

Grabbing a supermarket carrier bag she'd found on the floor, Kirsty started shoveling the cash into it as Jamie watched with a glazed face. "We'll sort out your share later," she told him.

Later, once she'd scrambled into a fresh pair of jeans she always kept at the club, she rejoined Jamie and they left the club by the back door.

When they were outside, Kirsty took one last look at the place. Then she hacked up as much spit as she could manage and with a flourish deposited it on the dirt outside the club. "Shit-hole," she shrieked.

Jamie shook his head. She ignored him. If she'd been a lady tonight she'd have been raped by a thug. Screw being a lady. Ladies got raped and dumped in ditches. That was not going to happen to her.

Once they'd walked away from the club, she told Jamie to give her a few minutes and crossed the road. She pulled out the envelope she'd put most of the money inside and shoved it in the post box. She'd pinched the pre-paid envelope from the office when Jamie wasn't looking and scribbled the address down in the toilets. It would have been suicide to carry that amount of cash around with her, considering what she was about to do.

She shoved the gun down the front of her jeans as she'd seen them do in the movies. She wasn't stupid. She knew she was going to need it.

"What were you doing?" Jamie asked when she rejoined him.

"Just getting prepared for war."

Four

JIMMY MCPHEE WAS PISSED OFF. Not only had the one-legged fancy piece brained one of his best men and buggered off with his money, she'd waltzed off with the gun that was so hot it was smoldering. As a precaution, the serial number was already filed off the revolver (he wasn't some dumb ass novice), but with the fancy Dan forensic techniques the polis used these days, the piece could still be linked with the murders. Including of one of the filth: a dirty cop, who'd been on Jimmy's payroll until the bastard developed a conscience and threatened to spill his guts.

O'Brien's bosses didn't know he'd ended up with a slug in the brain, executed after hours of meaningless torture before the sack of shit had been flung in the Clyde, a river that seldom gave up her secrets; not when you weighed down a body with chains and bricks. Jimmy's boys were a dab hand at the old disposal biz. So good in fact, they contracted their services out. There were a load of bodies to be disposed of in these parts.

What really made Jimmy want to stick the head on the next person to look at him the wrong way, wasn't just that he'd been done over by a bird with one bloody leg. Naw, it was the thought of having to arrange a meeting with his bitter cow of an ex-wife. Nan had gone all bunny boiler on him after he'd traded her in for a younger, more impressive model with nicer tits and a face not showing signs of ageing. Stupid cow should have seen the writing on the wall when he stopped asking her for blow jobs. Where the fuck did she think he was getting them from? The 15-year-old girl he was with now served all his needs. And there were plenty more where she came from. Jimmy had security contracts with most of the schools in Glasgow.

He picked up the phone, surprised to see his nicotine stained hands were shaking. One of his top guys Danny Boy, who knew when to notice things and when not to, stepped back and stood over at the window. McPhee dialed.

"Nan, it's me," he barked into the mouthpiece.

His introduction was met by a litany of abuse about what a fucker he was and numerous threats of violence against his person – Nan had always been a sadistic bitch – but he ignored her rants, saying,' yeah, yeah, yeah." Old news. Every last foul mouthed rant of it. The woman was a stuck record. Should have put a bullet in her brain when he'd had the chance.

When the abuse finally let up and he got a word in edgeways, they arranged a meet on neutral territory. There was something they needed to deal with or they were both screwed.

By the time he'd told her what was what, the bitch agreed.

As he headed out the door, he told Danny Boy to get him that stab proof vest. He wouldn't put it past the bitch to stab him with a rusty blade. She'd already taken one to his brand new Range Rover, so it was best to take precautions.

Bitch was as crazy as a bag full of rabid monkeys.

Five

WHEN KIRSTY TOLD JAMIE she was going to see Nan McPhee, she thought all the air was going to deflate out of him like a balloon.

"Why would you do that? Don't you think she'll hand you over to her husband?"

Kirsty shook her head, "No I don't. He screwed around on her and went off with a schoolgirl. Trust me, she hates his guts. One night at the club, she stabbed him with a fork." She laughed at the memory of McPhee jumping up and down, a human jack the box.

Jamie eyed her warily. "What if you're wrong?"

"Well," she said, with a faint smile, "I might not be around to hear you say you told me so."

A flicker of a grin crossed his lips. "You're a law unto yourself. Do you know that?"

She chuckled. "A right force of nature." Then turned serious. "You'd better go and hide out somewhere."

"But, what about my share of the money? I'm going to need some cash."

She blinked. His share? He'd acted as though he didn't want to soil his dainty wee hands with the dosh. But she could see why he'd change his mind. You needed money to be anonymous in this city. They were eyes and ears everywhere and only cash could buy their silence.

She stuck her hand down the front of her bra and pulled out a few rolls of notes that she hadn't put in the envelope and posted to her safety deposit box. She clocked his greedy little eyes knowing that they were as much for her breasts as for the money. He held out a hand and she gave him the cash. The money was still warm.

"Good luck," he'd said as they parted.

She watched him leave without looking back. Deep down in the pit of her stomach, her gut twitched. That's when she realized she would miss having him around.

● ● ●

Nan McPhee lived in a smart bungalow in Bishopbriggs, on the outskirts of Glasgow. To all her neighbors she may have been just another ageing divorcee on the wrong side of fifty, trying in vain to keep the years at bay with a private gym membership and countless sessions of Botox. Not that anyone dared tell her that because there was a cold menace about her no one could quite put their little pinkie on. And those who knew her knew she was one of the most feared folk in Glasgow with more than a few coppers in her back pocket and lucrative "business ventures" extending way beyond her husband's enterprises.

McPhee had let her have her "Wee sidelines' when they were married because he was too stupid to realize she was better at this game than he was. Nan had a reputation for being more ruthless than Jimmy, but some suckers stupidly believed she was the soft touch, no doubt because she was a woman. The truth was she had bigger balls than any man, as anyone would discover if they pissed her off. Kirsty had heard enough tales to justify that reputation.

Kirsty knocked on the door and waited, fighting the urge to run like the clappers in a risky game of chappie. The door swung open and a Goliath of a man appeared in the doorway, peering down at Kirsty as if she were an insect he'd caught in his jam jar that he was going to dissect with a penknife.

"I've come to see Nan. Is she in?" said Kirsty, leaning on her good leg and trying not to sound too much like a wee lassie asking if her pal was coming out to play. Large scary bastards tended to have that effect on her, especially when they had gargoyle faces.

Goliath nodded to her breasts. His expression was of someone who wanted to stick his head between her cleavage and go bluwwww before he fucked her with a steak knife and skinned her alive.

The man mountain grunted and lumbered aside. The whole floor shook. Kirsty resisted the temptation to ask him if he talked. She didn't want him to reach down into her throat and rip out her tongue and eat it on a piece like a slice of ham.

As she stepped inside she took one last glance at the leafy suburb. "Goodbye trees. Goodbye grass. Goodbye sky," she mumbled to herself, hoping she would get to see their likes again. Whether she would or not, was anybody's guess. She was aware that she was about to enter the monster's lair and that some people didn't make it out of this house alive.

The door swung shut with a thud and she was swallowed up by a shag pile carpet her feet disappeared into as she walked. In different circumstances she would have taken off her shoes and sunk her feet into its softness. It must have cost a bundle.

Goliath led her down a long hallway that was decorated with old black and white photographs of movie stars. Rita Hayworth, Marilyn Monroe, James Stewart, Humphrey Bogart and Greta Garbo stared back at her. Maybe this wasn't going to be so bad after all. Someone with a good taste in movies couldn't be all the bad. Must keep telling herself that.

When they came to the end of the hall, there were three doors. Goliath nudged her towards one and motioned with his huge head for her to enter. She took a deep breath and walked through the door.

The delicious aroma of home baking greeted her the second she walked into the kitchen. A woman was leaning over a fancy range stove. When Kirsty got closer she realized she was checking on some scones and rock buns. They smelt amazing and she tried hard not to salivate. This wasn't the time to be sidetracked by hunger, but the last thing she'd eaten was a plate of cereal some hours ago and she was starving.

The woman straightened up as she approached and Kirsty could see she was wearing a wedding ring with a rock the size of a meteorite. The diamond gleamed as the sun came in through the kitchen window. Kirsty wanted a rock like that one day, but not the same way Nan got it. Imagine having to bump uglies with Jimmy McPhee. The world didn't have enough carbolic soap to scrub you clean afterwards.

Nan caught her eyeing the ring. "When I married, I meant the 'to death do us part' bit. Unfortunately, Jimmy didn't agree."

She sounded sad, whimsical even and Kirsty frowned, trying to show sympathy she didn't feel. The woman was a cold-blooded psychopath. She couldn't do the things she did and have feelings.

Nan McPhee was a handsome woman with strong

features and an air of self-confidence. Her hair was honey blonde and her skin glowed courtesy of a spray tan that was almost natural and she had dazzling, white straight teeth, the legacy of some expensive orthodontics any Hollywood star would have envied. Even in a pair of jeans and a white blouse just visible under her apron, she oozed class.

Why did she marry an ugly weasel like McPhee? Must have been the money and the joint love for sadistic violence.

Taking a plate out of an overhead cupboard, she deposited two of the scones that were cooling on a wire rack on one of the granite topped units. When Goliath tried to pick up one, she slapped away his enormous fingers and he dropped it.

"They're for guests, Gregor."

He jumped back as though he'd been burnt and went to stand in a corner.

Nan motioned for Kirsty to sit at the solid oak kitchen table large enough to be used for dinner parties and set about preparing some scones for her guest, producing a tray full of different jams that she placed on the table. As she pottered about, she hummed away to herself.

When Nan finally spoke, it was to ask if Kirsty if she wanted a cup of tea. Kirsty's unease was growing. What the hell was the old Mother Hubbard act all about? Mrs Psycho didn't come over all motherly when you screwed her husband over. Not even when she hated the bastard and tried to chop his dangle bag off with a rusty axe – or so another story went.

But then Kirsty was hungry, so it was time to stop thinking and to start eating. She ate greedily, fortifying herself against the shit storm that was going to rain down on her from upon high.

As she ate, Nan carried on moving about in the kitchen, opening the oven and arranging things in the cupboards as if she was alone.

When Kirsty wiped the last remnants of crumbs and jam from her lips, she felt Nan's steely gaze upon her. Goliath was now positioned behind her back hungrily posturing; an attack dog about to be let off the leash.

"Who are you and what do you want?" said Nan.

So Kirsty told her about what the events at the club, failing to mention the money and the gun. Well, every girl needs her secrets. Nan stood there still as a lump of clay waiting to be molded, not moving or saying a word.

Once Kirsty had finished, Nan met her eyes with a steady gaze. "Why do you think I'll help you?"

"Because you hate your husband and want him to pay for what he did to you. What better way to piss him off than helping the barmaid who made a mug out of him?"

Nan gave that some thought, then tapped her nose with a well manicured nail. "Right enough," she said, "But I want a favor."

"Anything," said Kirsty. For once she meant it.

With an earnest look on her face Nan said, "Have a baby for me."

Kirsty's first reaction was "What the hell?"

But, she somehow managed to keep that to herself.

Six

KIRSTY SWALLOWED. Had she heard right?

"I can't have kids," said Nan. "I always thought it was because Jimmy didn't have the necessary lead in his pencil (she said it with a scowl), but a few years back I got tested and there's a problem with me too. I tried to adopt, but that fucker was having none of it. Sabotaged any chance we had of going legit. Nobody's selling babies in this country anymore." She broke off to make a face. "Too risky apparently. A surrogate was lined up, but she turned down my proposal to pay off her debts and ended up going the wrong way off a multi-story car park instead." Her face twitched. "She was pregnant at the time. Selfish wee cow."

Kirsty listened to this, trying to take it all in and not show the madwoman she knew she was a madwoman. That meant asking questions when she didn't give a monkey's what the answer was because she wasn't having this crazy bitches baby. First chance she got she was out of there with bells on.

"What would I have to do?" Kirsty said in a business-like

manner hoping it'd have Nan fooled. In her experience, the thing about crazy people is that they thought everything they did was rational and as long as you played along they seldom suspected you knew they were an out and out loony tunes.

Nan sat down on one of the chairs at the table and faced Kirsty. There was a faint smile on her lips, the kind you reserve for the bank manager when you're discussing a big loan. "I've got some cryopreserved sperm from an exclusive private clinic in Switzerland and I want you to be my surrogate." She paused and a proud smile crossed her lips. "Did you know it came from a 6ft 2 blonde, Swedish athlete with a PhD in Physics? They'll be no ugly wee runts surgically sewn into their tracksuits and trainers for me."

"So how do we get the sperm into me?" Kirsty knew the answer, but she was playing for time. Humoring the fruit loop.

"We use a syringe, of course."

Kirsty's braced herself in the chair, feet planted firmly on the floor so she'd be ready to run as if Jimmy McPhee himself were in the room armed with a machine gun. Time to ask the question Nan would expect. The one that could get Kirsty killed on the spot.

"What if we go ahead and I decide to keep the baby?"

"I'll cut it out of your stomach myself."

The words were delivered without venom.

Okay. Kirsty shifted in her chair, mentally sizing up the situation, weighing up the odds of making it out of here without the she devil's spawn inside her. Her placid face hid her fear that ticked inside her like an annoying clock. "If I do this you'll help me get away from Jimmy?"

Nan nodded. "You have my word."

Kirsty moved her lips, but no sound came out. She wanted

to give the appearance of mulling it over. Time for the killer question. The one she'd base her next actions on.

"I don't understand how you can guarantee I will hand over the baby."

Nan's lips puckered. "Until you have the baby, you'll stay at my villa in Marbella."

Fuck, she even had this all planned out, thought Kirsty.

Nan rattled on. "With company of course, but you will have certain freedoms. Treat it like a holiday. Go shopping, have dinner in fancy restaurants. Take in some sun. Not too much though, because that's not good for the baby. And no drinking. Don't want to end up with a baby with stunted growth."

"*The baby.*" Already she was talking as though it was a living, breathing thing and not a maybe in her fridge.

Spain wouldn't be a holiday, it'd be hell. Wherever she stayed would be a prison with someone watching her every move. There'd probably be bars on the windows and a rail to handcuff her to the bed when she went into labor. Well, they wouldn't risk taking her to a hospital. Too many awkward questions. A chance she might flee with the golden fucking egg.

And, what if she lost the baby? The psycho would cut her stomach open and throw what was inside to wild, ravenous dogs. If she was lucky.

Taking a deep, lingering breath, Kirsty tried to work out her play here, but all she could think was to say, "Can I get some time to think about this?"

Nan got up and walked over to a shelf where she picked up an egg timer. She wound it, making sure her visitor could see. "You have until this goes off."

This woman was one mad bitch and even if Kirsty had been the kind of woman to sell her baby, there was no way in hell she could trust Nan to keep her side of the bargain. A dead woman couldn't make any trouble.

Kirsty met her gaze. "I've thought about your kind offer and I have one main concern."

"Oh," said Nan. "What's that?"

"Why the hell would I have a baby for you?"

Kirsty flung her body at the wire rack where the baking was cooling and chucked it at Nan, narrowly missing her head. McPhee's missus acted as though she was brushing away a crumb.

"Now that was rude." There was disappointment in her voice; the kind a parent has for a child who has let them down in some way. Then she shouted, "Get her Gregor."

Kirsty sprinted for the door and had one hand on the handle when her other arm was wrenched back. She screamed in pain and frustration as Gregor put her in a bear hug and lifted her back towards the table. She swung her good leg backwards and thumped him hard on the knee. The bastard must have been made of granite, because he didn't even react.

She tried swinging her head back to give him a reverse Glasgow kiss, but she barely came up to his chest and her head hit solid muscle.

As she was carried over to the table, the gun dislodged from her waistband and she watched despairingly as it trundled to the floor. Nan retrieved it, dropping it in her apron pocket as though it were a stray spoon.

"Young people these days don't know how to behave," said Nan, straightening out a tug in her hair before bending down to pick up the scattered buns.

When she finished, she looked over at Gregor who was holding Kirsty in his best impersonation of a human seatbelt. "Now what to do?'" she said softly. "Oh I know. Hold her down on the table."

She swiped the palm of her hand along the table where a minute before Kirsty was eating her scones. The jam and plates spun off the table and clattered onto the floor tiles. With Gregor momentarily distracted by a half filled cup that bounced past his giant head, Kirsty seized her chance and went limp in his arms. He let her go, expecting her to fall onto the table. She did, but instead of just lying there she brought up her leg and landed on her bum.

Grabbing the knife she'd hidden in her sock, she yelled, "I'm getting out of here now. Try and stop me and I'll cut you up. Not that you could look any uglier." She nodded towards Gregor.

Kirsty backed away towards the door, all the time waving the knife wildly in front of her; relying on the hope Nan wouldn't want to shoot her.

For once Gregor and Nan were stunned into inactivity. Then Nan scream of "get her," dragged the henchman out of his dumb stupor.

As Gregor clumped towards her, vacant eyes staring dumbly at the blade as though caught in its thrall, she thrust out the knife and caught him across one of his hands. He stood transfixed by the sight of his own blood trickling down his hand, as if it was this miraculous thing. He hadn't uttered so much as a grunt.

Kirsty was so captivated by the giant's reaction she didn't see Nan with the gun. First she knew was when the crime matriarch screeched, "Stop, or I'll blow a hole in you."

Kirsty ignored her and kept on going out towards the hall, figuring Nan wouldn't want to risk killing her rent-a-womb. A bullet whizzed past her head, shattering a decorative plate on the wall and she ducked as shards of plate rained down on her.

"I'm a good shot," she heard Nan yell. "And you can still

have my baby even if I shoot you in the arm."

As if to demonstrate, she fired again. This time the bullet pinged inches past Kirsty's wrist. That stopped her dead in her tracks. Next time she could aim at her spine. Easier to keep a crippled surrogate from running off and taking a tumble off a multi-storey car park.

Kirsty held up her hands in surrender, letting the knife fall to the floor as she turned to face Nan.

"Let's head back into the kitchen shall we," Nan said, motioning with the gun. Kirsty didn't argue. She knew the damage guns could do.

Once they were back in the kitchen, Nan ordered her to lie down on the table. Kirsty ignored her and stayed standing. No way was she lying down. Let the cow shoot her. It was preferable to having the sick witch's baby.

She was going to tell Nan that. To spit it in her face when a blow from Gregor knocked her off her feet. The blow split her lip and she tasted the salt of blood as she staggered backwards, leaning against Gregor because he was the only thing keeping her upright.

Gregor caught her and flung her across the table. Electric shocks coursed through her spine as she landed on her back on the cold table. His huge frame loomed over her torso as he stood astride her, pressing her arms down with a pincer grip.

But that wasn't the most terrifying thing. As she writhed like a snake in an attempt to get free, she could see Nan with an insane expression on her face, holding a small cool box. Nan lifted up the lid and removed a small vial of a substance resembling watered down milk and inserted a syringe into the end. The syringe was ridiculously long and reminded Kirsty of the ones Matron Hattie Jacques wielded in Carry on Doctor.

The thought almost made her chuckle, but she'd have needed to be demented to laugh right now as Nan strode towards her singing "Daisy, Daisy, give me your answer do. I'm half crazy all for the love of you…"

"You are kidding," said Kirsty, noticing the shriek in her voice that seemed to come from a long way off.

Nan was holding the syringe. There was a mad glint in her eye, but with Kirsty kicking there was no way she could get her jeans and pants down far enough to do the deed. The problem was soon solved when Nan called for someone.

A blonde haired, blue eyed, too pretty girl appeared in the doorway. She gawped at the scene awaiting her.

"Well don't just stand there, Manika," said Nan. "Hold down her legs."

The girl obediently trotted over and ignoring the "don't you dare" warning fired her way, grabbed Kirsty's ankles. For her size she was surprising strong. She didn't even react when she felt the prosthetic limb.

Nan caught Kirsty's gaze and a "ha" crossed her lips. "Manika would have a baby for me, but back in her home country she was raped with a gun and it tore her up inside. Isn't that right girl?" Manika nodded; eyes small and beady like a mannequin's. "Now she works for me cleaning this house, but she will make a great nanny for my baby. Don't you think?"

Kirsty's mouth was full of curses. But, why waste energy on them now? *Need to get out of this. Somehow.*

There was a stool next to the table and McPhee deposited the syringe there and was unbuttoning Kirsty's jeans when her captive decided to try play nice.

"Okay, okay," said Kirsty. "You don't need to hold me down. I'll do it."

She tried to sound apologetic, which wasn't easy for her.

Kirsty McLeod never apologized, not even when she knew she was in the wrong. Sorry was for wimps. As was surrender.

"If I do this you will help me get away from Jimmy?"

Better to make it sound as if she was agreeing to a deal.

"You have my word," said Nan, with the same light tone she'd used to ask Kirsty if she wanted some tea. She instructed Gregor and the girl to let her go. "We can do this the civilized way."

Kirsty sat up as though she was going to pull down her clothes, but instead she jumped up and grabbed the pot bubbling away on the stove. She threw the steel pot at Gregor as he lurched towards her. He howled as the scalding water sizzled on his skin. Kirsty battery rammed Nan out the way and lunged for the door.

The girl was standing in her way, but made no move towards her. A small smile was dancing across her lips and she held what appeared to be a kid's yellow toy gun. Kirsty almost smiled back at her. Stupid cow. What was she playing at?

Then the cow pressed something and two strings of brilliant blue light with darts at the end came from the contraption and hit Kirsty square in the chest and she was writhing on the ground as cramp screamed through her entire body. She tried to lift herself up, drag herself to her feet, but she couldn't move as every muscle in her body contracted and contorted.

As fifty-thousand volts of electricity rendered her immobile, she vowed she would smash every last tooth in that little cow's perfect mouth and then make her eat them one by one.

Seven

BY THE TIME KIRSTY had regained the power of speech, she was flat on her back on the table with Gregor and the girl holding her down. She glared at Nan. "If you try and impregnate me again, I will kill the baby. I know how to do that."

Resignation swept across Nan's hardened face. "I can tell this isn't going to work."

With a crazed look, she threw the syringe across the room, muttering away about not being able to put it back. "See what you made me do."

Kirsty studied Gregor. His face was blank. Few thoughts registered in that thick skull of his. Kirsty could tell. The wheels turning, but nothing was happening.

"Take her down to the cellar and teach her some manners," Nan instructed him. She grabbed a huge knife from one of the chopping blocks and with a flourish of a smile, said, "Here's a wee toy to help things along."

She took Kirsty's gun out of her pocket and handed it to Gregor. "This is to finish her off, once you're done." Then for

Kirsty's benefit she said, "If there's anything left of the back-stabbing bitch."

Gregor hauled Kirsty off the table and pulled her into an upright position. She struggled to regain her balance, failed and he dragged her back to her feet nearly pulling her arm out of its socket.

He was marching her out the kitchen when Nan raised a hand. "Wait." She stomped over to Kirsty, and head-butted her full in the face. As Kirsty fell back into Gregor, reeling from the blow that brought tears to her eyes, Nan sneered. "Now, why couldn't you be nice? I'll need to find a new surrogate now."

Kirsty vowed there and then that if she ever got out of this cesspit alive she was going to bake Nan McPhee in one of her own pies.

Gregor shoved Kirsty out into the hall and made her walk in front of him. If she didn't move quickly enough, he jabbed her with the knife. At one point he stuck the blade into her ribs and she could feel the warm trickle of blood. Instead of wincing she spun round more than ready to tell him where he could stick his knife, but the glassy eyed stare he gave her forced her to think again. He was itching to gut her like a fish.

As she was marched towards the cellar, he said nothing. Kirsty kept her eyes peeled for a weapon. Anything she could use. So far there was nothing. She was screwed.

The door to the cellar was at the end of the hall. There was a keypad on the door. The numbers went from one to nine, which surprised Kirsty because she assumed the big lummox could only count up to three. Maybe the combination involved the few numbers he knew: 1, 2, and 3?

There was no time for her to think about it, because Gregor ignored the keypad and using his foot he kicked the door open. Before she could react, she was shoved in the back and was tumbling down stairs that went on forever.

There was no time for her to curl into a ball to limit the damage and she clobbered her head on a concrete step as she fell down and down, into the darkness. *Damn that hurt.* But at least she hadn't cracked her skull wide open as if it was a melon.

Dazed and feeling like someone had given her a right doing, she couldn't move as the clod of Gregor's footsteps headed her way. Then light flooded the darkness and the brightness hurt her head even more.

What she saw in the cellar scared the hell out of her. Suspended from the ceiling was a meat hook and it wasn't for Angus Beef. It was too high up for a start. Human being high.

As the big man advanced towards her, holding a yellow Taser out in front of him (*where the fuck did that come from*, thought Kirsty), making sure she saw it, she struggled to her feet.

Not again. The whimper erupting from her lips could have been from a wounded animal caught in a snare, not a fearless ass kicking bitch.

Gregor saw her fear and his lips got wider. He lurched towards her, feet like the Abominable Snowman, and there was nowhere for her to run. He was barring the only way in or out.

When he zapped her, the wind went out of her and the fight. She flopped onto the floor, screaming in agony with no control over her body; a puppet with someone else pulling the strings.

She could only watch as he forced her hands behind her back and snapped on handcuffs that had been lying on a crate. Then carried her like a sack of potatoes, over to a waiting chair and dumped her down.

Slowly, her senses began to return. Getting the feeling back in her body hurt as though every muscle, every tendon; every sinew of her had been over-stretched.

Gregor held the knife out so she could see it, teasing her with it. If he was trying to scare her he had another thing coming. Watching him galvanized her into action. No way was she going to play the mouse caught in his trap. Instead of quivering, she was a ball of fury, spitting, hissing at him, a wildcat.

"Cut me with that and I will hack your balls off and make you eat them," she raged.

No reaction. He brought the knife so close to her she could feel the coldness of the blade. See the glint of the metal as it danced across the pupils of his dull, grey eyes. He pressed it to her neck and she involuntary flinched. A grin danced across his lips and he licked them in anticipation of what he was about to do.

"Naw," he said, "cutting your throat's no fun."

His voice shocked her. She didn't think he could talk.

The size of his pupils reached gargoyle proportions as he sniffed her Hannibal Lecter style and said, "Let's play first wee lassie."

Kirsty face twisted in fury. The last man to call her "Wee lassie' ended up with his skull smashed into the porcelain of a toilet bowl, but she was in no position to ensure a repeat.

Gregor shoved his spade of a hand down her top and gripped her breast so hard in normal circumstances she would have screamed like a banshee. But she refused to show any weakness and bit back the "you bastard" that formed in her throat.

Her lack of reaction angered him and he poked the tip of the blade into her breast, drawing blood. This time she did scream. It bloody well hurt, but she felt stupid for showing weakness. It would only encourage the twisted bastard.

Gregor was going to stick the knife in her again when she lowered herself down to the floor so her head was now in line with the bulge in his trousers. He was getting excited. And when men got sexually excited they made mistakes.

"I bet this will be the nearest you get to a woman," she said softly, keeping a lid on her revulsion. If that thing came any closer she was going to bite it off. "The last time you were this close, you were coming out your ma and she had no say in the matter."

He didn't blink. Probably too dumb to understand the joke.

She opened her mouth wide and crudely circled her lips with her tongue in a way that her message could not be misunderstood. Not even by someone with half a brain.

This was her last throw of the dice before he stuck that knife in her intending to kill. Making it last for maximum pain.

He stared down at her. "Do it," he commanded.

He unbuckled his belt and let his trousers drop and the sight almost made her laugh. It wasn't the flaming tree trunk she'd expected, it was a cocktail sausage. So much for the size of a man's hands being an indicator.

"I can't do it with these handcuffs on," she said, expecting him to twig what she was planning. Instead he mumbled something and reached behind her back. There was a click as he unlocked the cuffs.

Pulling her hands in front of her, she rubbed them because they were starting to go numb. The bulge was bigger now and Gregor was standing there eyeing her hungrily. She kept the smile on her face as though she could think of nothing better than pleasuring him, but in her mind was somewhere else: planning how to get the knife he was holding or the gun in his pocket. No chance of the Taser; it was out of her reach.

Trying to hide the trembling in her fingers, because she knew this was the only chance she had to save herself, she put one hand in his pants and with the other yanked them down. She heard him whimper. As she grabbed his cock with two hands and tugged it lightly, she heard his breathing get faster and knew this was the time to pounce. She grabbed the knife hanging limply by his side.

By the time he noticed it was too late. Kirsty rammed the knife into his stomach above the groin. He squealed like a pig.

His gaze fell to where the knife was sticking out of his stomach. He staggered. That's when she grabbed the knife again and gave it an almighty twist until she heard something snap.

The whole floor shuddered as Gregor fell. His mouth was wide open, eyes bulging in their sockets. His giant hand swung wildly for the knife and missed. Then he went still.

Kirsty slumped down on the floor and tried to get her breath back. *An asthma attack was the last thing she needed.*

As she lay there, out of the corner of her eye she could see a brown sack. The kind they put potatoes in. But, whatever was in it wasn't vegetables. The sack was moving.

She paused for a moment, debating what to do. Her priority was to get out of here. Not get sidetracked. She was in enough trouble without looking for more. Anyone could be in there and if she let them out maybe they'd think she was somehow involved in them ending up in there and take their frustrations out on her. She'd had enough trouble raining down on her for one day.

But, what if someone needed her help? They could suffocate in there.

Curiosity and concern fought self-preservation and won.

Cautiously, she walked over to the bulging sack. It was tied firmly shut with rope. It took her a bit of work and a lot of swearing to loosen the knots.

The sack opened and a body fell out. The feet and hands were bound together with electrical wire.

She squinted when she realized who it was, not believing what she was seeing.

Under the gag she was sure the person was smiling.

Eight

JAMIE'S HEAD APPEARED to have been in collision with Mike Tyson's fist. His eyes were screwed shut reminding her of a puppy she'd once found tied in a sack and abandoned in a burn.

Slowly, he opened his eyes, trying to get accustomed to the light. The rims of his eyes were red and he was shivering. She removed the gag.

"It's you," he said. His voice so faint she strained to hear.

She went looking for a pair of pliers, suspecting there would be a pair lying around. Pliers were one of a Glasgow torturer's tools of choice after all.

She found a pair on the ledge under a bricked up window and quickly set about cutting away Jamie's bonds as he lay on the floor of the cellar. Whoever had bound him hadn't made a hellish good job of it, but Jamie still winced as she cut into the wire, perhaps fearing she'd hack off a bit of skin.

Once he was free and sitting up rubbing his hands, she stood towering over him.

"What the hell are you doing here, Jamie?" She tried to restrain the anger in her voice. She'd warned him to get out of Glasgow, but he'd defied her. Stupid bastard. Now he was a complication she didn't need.

What was she going to do with him? He was too old to dump on a church doorstep.

It might have been a trick of the light, but he grinned at her. "Nice to see you too," he rasped.

His voice was a whisper and she quickly scanned the room, hoping to find something he could drink. The best she could find was a half drunk bottle of whiskey; torturing was thirsty work. She handed him the bottle and he greedily gulped it down and quickly started to cough.

"What the hell was that?" he spluttered.

She ignored his question. There were more pressing matters to deal with.

"How the hell did you get in there?" Well, she had to ask. Sacks didn't tie themselves and jump into cellars.

"One of that crazy lady's thugs found me wandering about the garden and brought me here. Mad bastard had a Taser."

She nodded knowingly. But there was no time to compare war wounds. They needed to get a shift on.

She grabbed his arm. "We need to get the hell out of here. Can you walk?"

He threw off her arm and started walking.

They were half-way up the steps when he stopped and turned to her. "Can you do me a favor?"

"What?"

"Once we get out of here can you stay the hell away from me?"

"Should have left the gag in," she snapped back. "If this is how you show your gratitude."

"Gratitude? Jamie snorted. "Why should I thank you

when you got me into this shit?" How will I pay my rent now? I needed that job. I'll have to leave Glasgow now and go somewhere McPhee can't find me. All because you couldn't deal with a little attention. Just brilliant."

Kirsty held her hands out. "Okay, okay I hear you. I've been a naughty girl. Now can we cut the pity stuff and get out of here?" She motioned towards Gregor. "I think he's dead, but you can never be sure. I've had enough surprises to know."

"Okay," said Jamie through tight lips. "But, in case you don't realize, I came here to help you. Didn't think McPhee's missus was going to go all *Reservoir of Dogs* on me. That lady's nuts."

Kirsty gave him an earnest look. She didn't want to corrupt his school boy innocence, but he needed to know the harsh facts of life. "Did your mother never tell you, it's always the women you have to watch out for?"

"Too right," he muttered and began walking up the stairs.

Jamie was at the top when she called for him to wait, claiming she'd dropped her necklace. The gun was down there. She sprinted down the stairs.

Gregor was lying face down. Alive the brute must have weighed sixteen stone; dead he weighed twice that.

How was she going to move him?

The simplest solution would have been to ask for Jamie's help, but something made her reject that thought. That gun was her safety net. He didn't know about it and she wanted to keep it that way.

Tensing her arm, she reached under Gregor. Her arm hurt like hell, but somehow she managed to reach it. She put the gun in her pocket just as Jamie whispered that she needed to get a move on.

There was no one waiting for them on the other side of

the cellar door. Jamie led the way up through the house to the main door, tiptoeing like a kid hoping to snatch a glimpse of Santa on Christmas Eve.

When they got to the front door it was a relief to find the key in the door. Nan McPhee was careless about security in her lair. Maybe with Gregor about she didn't think she needed to take proper precautions.

When he opened the door, the chilly early morning air slapped them in the face like an ice queen's talons and Kirsty half expected a trio of Dobermans to come out of nowhere and tear them limb from limb. None appeared.

Out in the street they found a second wind from somewhere and jogged past the row of executive bungalows with huge SUV's and BMWs parked in the drives. They didn't stop until they came to a small park and slumped down on a bench. No one followed them, maybe because Nan assumed her pet Neanderthal was playing torture the barmaid in the cellar.

"Where to now, then?" asked Jamie. His color was returning.

Kirsty peered up at the sky with wonder. At one point she thought she would never see it again. "I have to go home."

Jamie's mouth was as wide as a whale's. "Are you off you head? That's the first place McPhee will look."

Of course she knew going home was sheer lunacy but she has things to take care of. Her dog for one. This was the day Mrs Torrance went to her friend Morag's, so she'd have dropped him off back at the flat after walking him.

There was another good reason she needed to go back to her flat - for her passport. She needed to get out of the country. It was the only way she wouldn't end up dead, face down in a ditch with her body showing signs of prolonged torture.

When she told Jamie why she was going to make the

dumbest move ever. he scrunched up his face, transforming him from choir boy to angry gang banger.

She jumped in before he could speak. "I know, it's the first place they'll look and it's stupid going back, but I have to see Benjy is okay. And I need a passport. Even with cash there's no guarantee I can get a dodgy passport in Glasgow without someone grassing me up to McPhee. He owns this bloody city."

He thought she was a whack job for even considering it. "I can understand you going back for the passport, but risking your life for a dog!"

But, he wasn't going to change her mind. No man ever changed Kirsty's mind. They tried, sure, with their fancy words and promises. But none succeeded.

Fighting back the urge to stick the head on him for insulting the one man in her life she could genuinely trust, Kirsty told him she was going, red hair trailing in the breeze.

When he gave her yet another disapproving look, she said, "I'll give you your share of the cash and you can go, then? Go anywhere you like."

He frowned. "I would never leave a damsel in distress."

He'd learn, thought Kirsty.

They walked until they came to the main road and Kirsty flagged down a black cab.

It wasn't until Kirsty sat down and inspected herself in the mirror she realized how bad she looked. An angry blue bruise was starting to form under one eye and the cut on her lip was impressive enough to grace any champion bout. The lip was already starting to go numb, so she wouldn't be kissing many sailors. Spiders' webs were running down her cheeks - not even waterproof mascara could survive a day like this - and her face resembled one of those kids who were forced to go down mines: all pale and wane, like sunlight was a luxury. In other words, like any other Glaswegian gal once they'd drunk a few.

Seeing her disheveled state almost made her scream at the taxi driver to take them to the nearest chemist so she could buy make-up to repair some of the damage. But she resisted. Jamie wouldn't understand. No man understood what it was like for a woman to go without her makeup, especially at a time when a girl needed all the confidence she could get.

"A bad night, eh?" said the taxi driver, eyeing her in the mirror. They both grunted and exchanged knowing glances.

As they drove across the city, Kirsty's mind terrorized her with all sorts of possibilities of what she'd find when she got home, because surely McPhee's muscle would have paid her a visit once they found the body and figured out who the doer was. She vowed there and then that if McPhee's louts had so much as touched a hair on her dog's head, she was going to go all Die Hard on their backside, even if it killed her.

Nine

THEY WERE A MILE AWAY from her tenement flat when they saw the first clouds of ugly black smoke belching into the Glasgow sky. Kirsty wanted to believe the smoke was nothing to do with her building; pure coincidence. Or, just some kids setting fire to the bin rooms. But the closer they got the sicker her stomach got.

Even before the driver turned the corner and drove into the street – Kirsty ordered him to drive slowly because she had to keep an eye our for trouble - she knew what they would find, but the sight that greeted her hurt like someone had reached inside her chest and gripped her heart.

Her whole building was on fire.

Three fire engines were parked across from her building with all personnel attending the blaze. Not that there seemed much point. Anyone could tell the building was a goner: the roof was buckling.

Behind a police cordon were people she recognized even if she didn't know their names, their faces a mixture of pain and bewilderment. Some were openly weeping. One little girl in her pajamas, stood clutching her rag doll, as her mother held her close to her chest, muttering reassurances Kirsty couldn't hear.

Kirsty pushed herself through the small crowd and to the front, recognizing more neighbors as she went. There was Mrs Shearer from downstairs, a stuck up cow who reminded her of Shrek. She was pale now and her enormous head appeared to have shrunk; she was so lost in her thoughts she didn't even acknowledge Kirsty's approach. When Kirsty got closer she could see the old woman was mumbling to herself, something about forgetting to renew her insurance.

Old Mr. McEwen from along the hall was standing gripping his wife's hand, his face a mask. His dementia suffering wife stood with the wide-eyed innocence of a child, flames dancing in her pupils like lights from birthday candles. She was singing "London's Burning" in a child's voice that creeped Kirsty out.

Guilt overwhelmed her. She was responsible for bringing this to their door.

The consequences of her actions and the effect on others weighed her down like the stone necklace McPhee's thugs would have put on her to weigh her body down in the Clyde.

McPhee's heavies must have started the fire. They had form. They'd done the same thing to families who owed him money. Petrol soaked newspapers shoved through letterboxes, followed by a match. The police knew it was done at McPhee's bidding, but they could never make charges stick, not even when they caught the perpetrators. To even so much as hint at McPhee's involvement was to say you wanted a psycho to take a power drill to your head, or if you were lucky your kneecaps. Even if anyone did squeal, there were enough bent coppers with deep pockets to make any charges stick.

Standing there, watching her building being consumed by the flames, she was certain the one person she wanted to see was not there. Their absence made her feel empty inside and she was sure if she tried to speak it would come out as a croak. *Where was Benjy?* They seemed to have evacuated the building and those nearby; surely they'd have found him and given him to one of the neighbors to take care of? Scanning the crowd, he was nowhere to be seen.

Right there and then, she vowed that if he was hurt she was going to get a power drill and ram it up McPhee's backside; with the thing still switched on.

She lunged towards the front of the tape. She needed to tell the firemen to find her dog. A policewoman appeared and ordered her to stand back. Ignoring her, she tried to duck under the tape but another constable appeared and together they manhandled her back behind the line.

"My dog," she said. "You have to find my dog. He's in there." She pointed to the top floor flat where the worst of the fire was. "Please."

The police officers exchanged worried glances. It was the PC who spoke. "As far as we know miss, the whole building was evacuated. The Fire Brigade would have brought out your dog if they'd found him." The if hung in the air, as she choked back the tears.

She tried to run past them again and they grabbed her. "If you try that again miss, we'll have to arrest you."

It was the woman PC who spoke this time. Her pompous manner made Kirsty want to deck her and her fists clenched in preparation. But she stopped herself in time. If she got locked up she wouldn't find Benjy and the McPhees would find a way of getting to her, wherever she was.

She walked away from the cordon. She would go in the back way without them seeing.

"Kirsty." She heard Jamie's voice behind her, but she ignored it and kept on walking. If he knew what she was planning he'd try and stop her. At that moment, she could do without his attitude.

She was walking on when she heard an excited woof.

She pivoted round in time to keep her footing as Benjy cannoned into her, his tail going like the blade of a helicopter's. He jumped into her arms and his hot wet tongue licked her face. In normal circumstances she would have ordered him to get down, but this time she lapped it up, clapping him and telling him what a "good boy" he was and how much she'd missed him as she planted kisses on his head.

Mrs Torrance let out a little shriek of delight when she saw Kirsty. The smile lit up her face. "I was so worried about you. I thought you were in the building."

Kirsty flung her arms around the woman. Not prone to public displays of emotion, Mrs Torrance hugged her right back.

"Thanks for taking care of Benjy."

Mrs Torrance beamed. "That's all right dear."

Kirsty was confused. "I don't understand though why he was with you. You usually drop him off at mine's."

Mrs Torrance wrinkled her nose. "I was going to, but then I saw two unsavory types going up to the stairs ahead of me. So I brought Benjy back with me."

Kirsty ruffled Benjy's ears. "Mrs Torrance, I have one favor to ask."

"Yes, dear."

"Can you look after Benjy for a while? There's something I need to do I'll come and get him when I can."

"Are you in some kind of trouble dear?"

Kirsty put on a smile so fake it should have been on a politician's lips. "I have to take care of some business that's all."

Mrs. T frowned, and then nodded. "Of course I'll look after him."

Kirsty knelt down and kissed Benjy on his square forehead framed by two odd shaped ears. He showed his appreciation by licking the top of her hair. Then she pulled herself up. "I'll send you some money when I can."

Mrs Torrance put Benjy back on his lead. "Don't worry dear. I won't let anything happen to him." Then turning to the dog she said, "Time for dinner Benjy. I have a pork chop with your name on it." And with a smile to Kirsty and an inquisitive glance towards Jamie, she was off, cantering down the street towards her house a few blocks away.

Kirsty watched them go with a heavy heart. *Behave*, she told herself. It wasn't as if she could take the dog with her.

Dragging all the air into her lungs, Kirsty exhaled and turned to face Jamie. "Where to now?"

She answered her own question. *How the hell did she know?* She was all out of options. She couldn't go to any of her friends – the few there were – because a, she didn't have many, and b, anyone she went to would end up with trouble at their door. No way did she want McPhee to burn their houses down.

Jamie deliberated for a moment, his face etched with concentration. Finally, he said, "I've got the keys to a student mate's place whilst he's on holiday. We could stay there. No one will be expecting to find you there."

"Okay," she said. There was nowhere else to go.

"His girlfriend might have some clothes you can borrow," Jamie added.

Kirsty reacted as if he'd spat in her face. "What you trying to say, buster?"

Jamie's faint smile faded faster than an erection after a kick in the balls. He moved back, his hands hanging loosely from his sides. "Sorry, I didn't mean…" His face flushed and his gaze dropped to the pavement.

A grin spread across her face. "Got you," she said, reaching across and playfully patting him on the arm.

Realization dawned and he relaxed his shoulders. "Aw right."

The grin left her face when she gazed down at her clothes. She was a right state. Her clothes were so grubby and torn even a tramp would have tossed them in a bin.

Dragging her fingers through her long hair, she knew she resembled the mad French woman who lived in the woods in Lost. Jamie was right. She did need to get cleaned up.

Ten

FOR A STUDENT PAD, Jamie's pal's pad was pretty swanky. Kirsty had expected a grotty student bed-sit with bed sheets as curtains (if there were any at all), in a darkened, musty room, stinking of decomposing takeaway and festering boxer shorts.

The reality surprised her. The apartment was an executive pad in a converted warehouse alongside the Clyde and not that far from the casino. Whoever this friend was, he must have had rich parents, or been some kind of big scale drug dealer. All expensive leather and glass furniture, the place was immaculate.

Flopping down on the huge couch, Kirsty eyed the biggest plasma telly in creation: it was about 60 inches wide. Someone was clearly compensating for having a small one.

"Wow," said Kirsty, taking it all in. "Sure your pal's no a Saudi prince?"

Jamie told her he was going to find her some clothes and scurried up the stairs. With him gone, Kirsty seized the opportunity to mull over recent events. She'd killed someone. Not that she felt any guilt – the guy belonged to an era where caveman roamed, grunting at one another and dragging their womenfolk into their caves by the hair where they'd ravage them.

As for Nan McPhee that woman was as mad as a bag of ferrets. Why the hell had Kirsty thought she would help her? It had been brainless. She was more dangerous than her ex-husband. He was a murdering psychopath. But she was on a different level entirely.

Jamie reappeared with a smug grin on his face. When he handed her a pile of clothes she understood why. It was a pink velour tracksuit, of the kind some bloody WAG would wear. She cut his grin dead with a scorching stare. He didn't even have the decency to flinch. He was no longer scared of her.

She took the clothes and headed upstairs to find the bedroom. Considering the state her current get up was in, anything would be preferable although she'd never gone through a pink stage: she'd gone straight to black.

The bedroom was as she suspected it might be: black satin sheets on the bed, mirrored ceilings. Its owner must think he was hot stuff in the bedroom. Either that or he was into making porn movies and getting the girls in his bed to audition, with or without their knowledge.

Kirsty had been there, done that, dished out the retribution and made him pay. It was amazing how apologetic men got when you had a knife and they were naked and tied to a bed.

When she opened the door of the cupboard to see if there were any trainers she could borrow, she found herself confronted by a collection of whips and chains. There was other sexual paraphernalia there too, including nipple clamps, huge dildos that looked almost comical and a row of blind-folds hung up so neatly they could have been ties. She was open-minded, but a stone settled in the pit of her stomach and stayed there. Something wasn't right.

She made a mental note to ask Jamie what this friend's parents did. She didn't have long to wait, because she heard movement behind her and turned round to see Jamie watching her.

"I see you've found the toys," he said. There was laughter in his voice.

She bristled. The door was shut and he hadn't even knocked. Was he trying to catch her naked?

She was about to ask him what he was doing, coming in without knocking when something stopped her saying anything. Call it a feeling, intuition, but suddenly she felt uneasy.

She did what she always did when she felt anxious, she cracked a funny. "Most men wait until at least the second date at least to show me that stuff."

"How do you…" He pointed to her leg. "When…"

She snapped back. "You mean do I keep my leg on?"

He nodded.

"My leg was amputated below the knee. I can do the stuff that most people can, like dancing and riding a bike. I can keep it on during sex or take it off. I do whatever comes naturally and usually keep it on." She paused and breathlessly said, "Anything else you want to know?"

Jamie shrugged. "Just curious."

Kirsty's body relaxed. "It's okay. I don't mind."

And off Jamie went with a funny look in his eyes that if Kirsty hadn't known better she would have interpreted as lust, but if he had feelings for her why hadn't made a move?

● ● ●

She was rummaging through the fridge, searching for something to eat, when she came across a jar of pickles amidst the pieces of silver foil containing the unmistakable aroma of hash. Pickles would help get rid of the nasty taste in her mouth. She unscrewed the jar and stuck two fingers in, pulling out a pickle dripping with juice. Tentatively, she lowered it into her mouth, taking great care to avoid touching her lips that still nipped from being punched in the face.

The pickle stung her tongue and made her eyes water, but it felt good, so she reached for another one and got the fright of her life.

The thing she'd plucked out of the jar wasn't a pickle. It was too long and thin for one thing and was weirdly familiar. She gasped when she felt a nail, then a ring.

When her brain fully registered what it was, she shrieked and the finger fell on the floor.

Eleven

KIRSTY BENT DOWN to get a closer look. This could not be happening. It'd been a bitch of a day, she'd been knocked around, almost artificially inseminated with a stranger's sperm, Tasered and then tortured, but no matter what was thrown at her they'd failed to knock all the fight out of her.

But, as she gazed down, she realized she hadn't been wrong: it was a finger.

The finger was small, slender and delicate, but too big to be a child's. A woman's finger. The French manicure was a giveaway. Unless it was a cross-dressing man, with perfectly manicured nails and small fingers. Very unlikely.

Kirsty laughed, shaking her head. This must be some kind of joke. There was no way it was real. Today was shitty enough without this being real.

Heart drumming a beat in her head, she reached out and touched the finger, expecting it to be made of rubber or latex, the same as her leg, or whatever they made fake fingers out of these days. But, it was no trick finger.

She yelped and pulled herself to her feet, which wasn't easy to do with a false leg. This could not be happening. She couldn't have stepped straight from a gangster flick into an American B horror movie.

What she was going to do now, she told herself as calmly as she could, was to pick the thing up (she couldn't bring herself to say finger), stick it back into the jar, scoot upstairs, grab the gun and run like a bastard.

She picked up a dishtowel and used it to pick up the finger and deposit it back in the jar. She wanted to pretend she'd never found the digit. There was nothing in the pickle jar, but pickles. Because if she admitted there was a human finger in a jar, she'd have to think about how it got there.

She was screwing on the lid when she heard Jamie's voice behind her.

"So, there you are."

She jumped and hoped he didn't notice. "Yeah, I was hungry. Hope your mate doesn't mind?" Her back was to him and she was praying he wouldn't come over, because if he did he would see the jar. Maybe want a pickle.

"No. Eat away. Doubt there's much in there anyway. He lives on takeaways."

Not so much as a flicker. *He can't know about the finger.* But, she needed to test him, to know for sure, so she slipped the jar back in the fridge and walked over to him, hips swaying.

"I know what you mean," she said with a forced cheer she didn't feel. "There was a moldy bit of cheese the mice wouldn't eat and a jar of pickles." She kept the tone light, studying him for a reaction. None came.

"I'll order in a takeaway," he said, as she strode past him, through the kitchen door, all the time wary of the fact that at any time he could pounce.

She made it passed him and was heading for the stairs when he shouted after her. "Kirsty."

Her heart skipped a beat and she turned round. "Yep."

"Pizza, okay?"

Relief slowed the pounding in her head. It was okay. He didn't know. If he did, surely he would have reacted?

She smiled at him. "Sure, that's great. Cheese and tomato for me, please. I'm going to lie down for a bit if you don't mind. Need to get my head straight."

She dragged herself upstairs to the bedroom, stopping halfway up the stairs. This was stupid. She should tell Jamie what she found. His friend was a nutter; maybe a serial killer. Didn't they keep souvenirs of their victims? Items they owned: clippings of their hair, body parts? She was pretty sure they did.

Jamie needed to be warned in case his pal tried to pin the crimes on him. Or, worse, added him to his list of victims.

But Kirsty was sick with hunger and that stopped him from blabbing. She could tell him later. Let him order the pizza first.

After positioning a heavy chair under the door handle to block entry and closing the blinds, Kirsty flopped down on the bed, too exhausted to appreciate how tacky this room was. Time for a nap before the grub arrived. She patted one of the pillows, felt the reassuring lump of the gun and sank down on the bed.

Her runaway train of a brain ground to a stuttering halt as tiredness overwhelmed her, but even in her dreams there was no escape. Someone was chasing her and she was breathless from running but she couldn't let up because it was over if she did: he'd kill her.

It wasn't until her assailant caught up with her that she realized the snarling man with the knife was Jamie.

Twelve

WHEN KIRSTY WOKE she didn't know where she was. Seeing her reflection in the mirror above the bed, wearing a ridiculous pink velour tracksuit brought it all back to her. She hauled herself out of bed and put the chair back where she'd found it, then headed down the stairs. The takeaway should have arrived by now.

Jamie was spread out on the couch, channel surfing. When he saw her, he smiled. "Good sleep?"

She rubbed her eyes, trying to adjust to the light. "Not bad, if you ignore the nightmares about mad bastards chasing me and trying to impregnate me with Rosemary's baby."

Jamie chuckled. He thought she was kidding.

Kirsty slumped down on the other couch. There was a takeaway carton lying on the glass coffee table. Jamie followed her gaze and pulled himself to his feet.

"The food came, but I didn't want to wake you," he said.

He went into the kitchen and she heard a microwave door being opened. A few minutes later there was a ping. She was already salivating as he walked in with the pizza. Thick crust, loads of cheese and freshly cut tomatoes oozing their juices onto the crust. She was in heaven as she dug in.

Once she was finished she wiped her chin with the back of her hand and met Jamie's gaze. "Jamie, how well do you know this pal of yours? What do his parents do for a living? I assume a student couldn't afford all this."

Jamie shrugged. "I'm not sure."

"They must be loaded. This place must have cost a fortune."

Jamie didn't answer and went back to watching the TV.

As she watched his eyes light up when he came to a Tom and Jerry cartoon, she came to a decision: she needed to tell him about her grisly find.

She took a deep breath and stood in front of the TV, blocking some of his view. "Do you have any idea why your friend's got a human finger in a jar of pickles?"

What struck her was the lack of surprise on Jamie's face. He knew about this.

He raised his eyes in a gesture she might have once found cute, if she hadn't seen some poor cow's finger in a pickle jar.

That's when the truth hit her full force in the face like a flying fist in a Glasgow pub: the reason he knew where everything was and was so damn comfy here, wasn't because his mate's place was a home from home. Nah, this was his home. She cursed herself for being so gullible.

She jumped up, ready to make a run for it but instead she eyed him.

"What the hell did you do?" She tried to hide the fear in her voice.

If he'd cut off some woman's finger, what had happened to the rest of her? When a nut job lopped off your finger, it's not like you wouldn't tell anyone. You'd go the police, screaming blue murder.

Right at that moment, as Jamie carried on watching as Jerry hit Tom over the head with a dustbin lid, there was an image in her mind of a woman's head in a freezer, along with other body parts.

Kirsty wanted to go over there and punch him. To demand to know what he'd done.

Instead, she said, "Did you kill her?"

He gave a wee smile.

"Who was she?"

That wee smile again, with no warmth behind it: just a chill that went all the way to her bones.

"Remember Melissa Hardy?" he said.

She gasped. The barmaid from McPhee's. She'd been working there to pay off her student loan. One night, she was a no show. Kirsty assumed she'd quit; any girl with common sense did. The tips were good at McPhee's, but there was too much pawing. Guy bought you a drink when you were on the bar, he thought he owned you. A smile at the wrong guy was a come on. A few times she had seen Melissa in floods of tears over the sexual harassment. Unlike Kirsty, she didn't know how to put the cavemen in their place with a swift boot in the bread basket.

"You've got a lot more to worry about than that tease, darling." Jamie's tone was mocking and he started beating a drum roll on the door. The sound grated, making her want to could take a hammer and smash all his fingers to pulp, one by one.

"Cue the drum roll…" he said.

She glared at him, full of loathing.

"I don't think I've introduced myself properly. I never told you my real surname, did I? It's McPhee. Jamie McPhee. I also go by the name Jamie Stewart, my mum's maiden name."

Kirsty blinked. This could not be true. He was messing

with her head. "You can't be. McPhee doesn't have a son. That's why his psycho witch of a wife wanted me to have her baby."

"He's my uncle," said Jamie proudly. Gone was the blue eyed innocence, replaced by a hardness in his features. He was no longer pretending to be nice guy Jamie; the innocent student caught up in a bad situation because he wanted to defend the girl he was sweet on.

This couldn't be right. This was too much like a bad script for a movie that would go straight to DVD.

Something else occurred to her. Maybe his answer to this question would trip him up, expose this as one big fib. "If you're McPhee's nephew why the hell would your own auntie put you in a sack?"

Jamie's face twisted with hate. "Bitch has never liked me. She couldn't give Uncle Jimmy a son and I'm as good as a son to him." He flicked his hand as if he was presenting himself on stage. "Uncle Jimmy's making sure I get the best education money could buy. He owns this place and set me up financially so I could attend university. He wants a lawyer in the family. But he needed someone he could trust to keep an eye on the club because some wide boy's been dipping his hands into the till. So, nice guy Jamie was born; everybody's friend, including the crippled slut."

He waved his hand as if to say "Turrah," and gave an exaggerated twirl. "And he's a right sweetheart. Aint he darling?"

On telly crime dramas this was the point where a character – usually the one who has a gun at their head – dumbly says: "What happens next?" But Kirsty was no dumb broad and this wasn't some crappy American detective show.

Without missing a beat, she ducked past Jamie and lunged for the stairs, heart pounding, and arms pumping like Usain Bolt. She had to get the gun. The element of surprise was hers and she'd made it halfway up the stairs before she heard him coming after her. He wasn't running, he was walking. His pounding footsteps on the stairs matched the pounding of her heart.

She got to the bedroom and threw herself at the gun hidden under her pillow and pointed it at Jamie who was standing in the doorway with a smug look. The gun was much heavier than she remembered.

She'd thought holding the gun, feeling the full weight of it in her hand would fill her with power, but instead she felt the responsibility of it; the burden and her whole body shook.

When it came to kicking the crap out of people she could more than hold her own, but handling a gun was like handling a pair of chopsticks: you might pretend you know what to do, but you'd be lying.

How the hell did you even fire the thing?

She needed to learn fast, because she was just as likely to shoot off her own toes as to kill him. And the bastard knew it.

He moved closer, an inquisitive expression in his face, head moving from side to side as if she was a puzzle he had to solve. "You point that gun at me and you'd better be prepared to use it, Kirsty."

There was no threat in what he said, simply a statement of fact.

Uncomfortable by his closeness to her, she stood her ground because to retreat would be as good as surrender. He would know her bottle had crashed. Then all the power would be his and this gun would be a useless object in her hand.

She kept her gaze steady. "Come any closer and I will shoot."

She tried to put some steel into her voice, straining to

control the uncertainty she felt, all the time trying to control her breathing. Trying not to sound as freaked out as she was.

Jamie glowered at her as if she were a piece of meat at a barbecue he wasn't sure was safe to eat. Then his features slackened and his lips curled up into a sneer.

"You're not going to fire, darling. Trust me, I've seen men who do and I know that look in their eyes. You don't have it."

"Oh yeah," she scowled. Pointing the gun at him, she used her other hand to steady her wrist as she'd seen them do on cop shows, and curled her finger around the trigger and pulled it back. Then she fired.

The fucker had called her darling once too often.

Thirteen

THE BULLET HIT HIS ARM. The gunshot reminded her of the sound of microwaveable popcorn popping.

Jamie howled and a crazed look spread over his once soft features. Dazed, Kirsty had expected exhilaration, instead she was numb. The gun fell limply to her side.

Eyes blazing with hatred, Jamie screamed "bitch" and hurled himself at her.

He was on her quicker than a Glaswegian in a drunken brawl, trying to yank the gun free by grabbing at her arm. Pain surged up the limb and the gun flew from her grasp and skidded across the carpet.

"Oh, shit," she mouthed, diving for the weapon. He was closer.

A sickening chuckle rose from his throat as he locked his fingers round the barrel, seemingly oblivious to the pain in his other arm. He stood up and raised the gun in triumph towards her as she lay helpless on the carpet, crawling away from him, desperately trying to haul herself up.

With a mad gleam in his eye, he spat, "You crazy bitch" into her face and clouted her on the side of the head with the butt of the gun.

Her brain screamed with pain as something warm and gooey ran down her face. And she was falling through air; a rag doll tossed aside by a spoilt brat. She landed with a resounding thud against a table, cracking her back against the heavy wood. But she felt no pain.

Her first thought was, *I'm paralyzed*. Her second thought, almost made her laugh like a lunatic in an asylum. Did it really matter, because she was dead anyway?

He strode towards her, gun pointing at her chest. He'd got a scarf from somewhere and it was tied around his arm to stench the bleeding.

"Any last words, Kirsty?" He hissed when he said her name; taking the piss.

"Screw you," she spat, her face set in a determined scowl. The heat of her rage was capable of vaporizing the room and everything in it.

"Now that's not very ladylike, especially from the girl I took home to meet my Auntie Nan." He was milking the moment.

She wanted to yell at him to fire and get it over with, but he wanted her to beg. Screw him.

She may have been lying in a crumpled heap, with blood streaming down her face, mixed in with tears and snot, but no way was she going to beg. She'd never beg. Not ever again.

"Jamie…" she said with forced hope in her voice.

"Yeah." His eyes were bright. He thought she was going to plead for her life. Probably getting a hard on as his mind went over the infinite possibilities of the indignities he could inflict upon her before he killed her.

"…go fuck yourself."

He fired and she felt a sharp sting. When she gazed down, there was a hole on the centre of one of her breasts. It smoldered.

"Damn," she screamed, not feeling any pain. "I love this top."

He scrutinized her, eyes filled with confusion, wondering why the bullet hadn't killed her. She used the confusion to wrench the gun from his hand and this time she held it out towards him with a steady hand. No need for her other hand to steady it this time. No way was she going to balls this one up.

His lips said "What the hell" but no sound came out. With the gun still trained on him, she reached down inside her bra and pulled out the bullet and held it out in her palm so he could see.

"Breast implants," she said, beaming. "Must have hit one of those puppies. Best money I've ever spent."

Holding the gun out, she aimed at something she doubted he possessed, a heart, coolly said "bang, bang your dead" and pulled the trigger.

The full force of the bullet propelled him through the air, his mouth contorted in pain; his eyes widened in a twisted parody of The Scream painting. He was hanging there, a scarecrow lifted by the wind, arms flapping in the breeze; eyes not quite human, staring at her. Then silence.

Nobody warned her about the silence. The way every-thing, went slow, as if she was picture searching, on a video, trying to rewind to a point in time, maybe before she discov-ered the finger and found out who and what Jamie was.

In his final moments, he was transformed back to being Jamie the barman and that surprised her. Why was she now seeing him in the mask he'd put on? At that moment, she almost unloaded the gun on his face, obliterating it. But she knew there weren't enough bullets for that. She could see there was only one bullet left in the chamber.

Dropping the gun to the floor, she walked over to where he was lying, eyes staring up at the ceiling as if admiring the stars. Something hot and sticky dripped onto her on the face and she casually flicked it off. It was only pulped bits of brain. Been there. Done that.

As she stood over him and watched the light in his eyes fade away, she said, "That's what you get for calling me darling."

Fourteen

KIRSTY SANK DOWN to the floor of the shower, hugging her knees to her chest and bawled her eyes out. The sudden outpouring of emotion crept up on her like some sex pest on a Glasgow bus.

After she'd killed Jamie, she'd been fine as she stripped off and climbed into the shower, desperate to scrub away the dirt of the day. But after a few minutes of luxuriating in the warmth, the reality of what she'd done swamped her and she was weeping, the way she'd vowed she never would again; until her throat was raw and she had a lump the size of a cue ball.

She tried to get herself to stop by digging her nails into the palm of her hand. She told herself to pull herself together and to stop being such a wuss. But, still the tears flowed and she couldn't work out why.

Would Jamie have cried for her? Not bloody likely. So, why was she crying for that treacherous piece of crap?

He was dead and she didn't regret pulling the trigger. It was him or her.

Then she realized: it was Jamie the barman she wept for, proof that not all men were vile bastards, until she realized he was just another lie; as bad as anyone she'd ever met. One woman was dead because of him. Were there more victims? Did he collect their body parts: a finger here, a pinkie there, a toe, a heart, a liver?

She didn't doubt there were more victims. The question was, were they in the past or the future?

What had he planned for her? She knew, but her mind wouldn't let her believe it. In the last 24 hours she'd put up with enough crap to last a lifetime. The prospect of her being a serial killer's target was one horror too far.

Time went on without her as she sat, huddled under the shower, until the water ran cold and her teeth chattered as if they were the wind up kind. She needed to get up, to put on her clothes and haul her backside out of here.

She pulled herself to her feet and immediately slumped back down again, dizzy, sick, a staggering drunk at chucking out time.

Five minutes later, she'd got a grip and with the gun safely back in her pocket, she left the flat.

If she was in a heap of trouble before she was in a shit load now. There was no time to wallow. Killing Jimmy McPhee's heir apparent was not going to go down well. He'd want her head on a stick. Bastard would need to find her first.

She considered going to the police and cutting a deal for all of five seconds – she knew enough about McPhee's business dealings to put names to faces – but she was well aware his sort only managed to operate in Glasgow because of the dirty cops in his back pocket. Before the case got to court, she would be found at the bottom of the Clyde with her pockets full of bricks. That's what happened to those who ratted on Glasgow's gang lords. If they were found at all.

There was another reason why going to the cops was a no, no. How could she explain away two murders? Kill once. Maybe they'd buy self-defense if they were too stupid to see that victim no.1 was death by stiletto. But, twice? No way.

What she needed was a new passport.

There was only one place to turn and she hated to go there, but there was no other choice.

Fifteen

SHE CAUGHT THE UNDERGROUND to Cessnock, all the time keeping an eye out to ensure she wasn't being followed. Jamie
could have alerted his uncle whilst she slept. For all she
knew, his thugs might be on her tail. But she didn't think so.
McPhee's Muppets weren't noted for being able to melt into
a crowd or their brains.

That's why she'd been able to get the better of one in
McPhee's bar. That and the fact the eejit let his cock do the
thinking for him. He wasn't the first man to do that, but he
was the dumbest.

Cessnock was the same shit-hole she remembered. Run
down tenement houses concertinaed together, full of newly
arrived Asian families with three generations living under
one roof in abject squalor. Recently they'd been joined by
Romanian immigrants and she wasn't surprised to see
young girls standing in doorways with what they thought
were come hither looks. They were dressed – if you could
call it that – in tiny halter neck tops that showed off their

undeveloped breasts and hot pants that would have show-cased womanly curves, but on young pre-pubescent girls were a kiddie fiddler's wet dream.

The place was turning into a down-market Amsterdam, the kiddie version and it sickened her. .

No one paid her any attention as she walked past them, doing her past to appear as if she belonged.

Swallowing her revulsion, she headed down a close. She ignored the first few houses with scuffed children's toys out-side and stopped at the fourth one on the right, rapping her knuckles five times on the grey metal door. Last time she'd been here, that was the code.

There was no answer after a minute so she knocked on the door again, this time loud enough to wake the dead. If he didn't open up soon she was going to come back with a blowtorch and open the door herself.

"Coming," she heard a familiar voice say. She was not in the mood to be kept waiting.

"Well come fucking quicker then," she hissed.

There was a raspy chuckle from behind the metal door and something was slid across the door, from the inside. The metal door swung open and a big dreadlocked head came into view. Kirsty took a deep breath.

"I knew it was you, my white queen," said Donald, with a grin that would have been toothy if he'd had many left.

He stood in the doorway, all six foot two of him. The Jamaica football shirt he wore hung off his skeletal frame. The man was a walking coat hanger. Crack cocaine had a tendency to do that to people.

Donald committed the dumb error of sampling his own merchandise. Kirsty warned him what would happen, but having "a leetle" occasionally, fast became having a lot, every day of the week. Hence his current state and her reluctance to seek him out earlier.

He motioned for her to come in. "Kirstee, you are looking as sexeee as ever."

Forcing a smile, she pushed out her boobs and hugged him. He didn't even try to cop a feel, which was so unlike him. Clearly the crack had snuffed out his sex drive.

Appealing to his better nature was the best bet. "Donald, I need you help." She chewed her lip after she said it, scarring her newly applied lipstick and hating herself for sounding so needy.

"Come into my office," he said, holding out his hand, his beam getting wider.

She followed him down the short hallway and past a shambling figure of indeterminate age or sex. The thing was humming away to itself, and they reeked of puke and pee. Kirsty pretended she couldn't smell it or the stink would have knocked her flat on her back.

There was a decrepit black leather couch in the living room (it looked as if someone got an attack of the munchies and tried to eat the stuffing) and a table covered in various drug paraphernalia. Seeing the dive Donald was living in, made her wonder whether she should have let McPhee and his boys kill him that night. It would have been a less agonizing exit than the one he was racing towards.

Back then she'd lied about seeing a police car heading their way and when McPhee and his thugs headed back to the club, Donald managed to drag himself away and hide in an alleyway where she'd discovered him hours later. He was lucky to escape with a concussion and a broken leg after he'd taken a kicking over an unpaid debt. Folk ended up having power drills drilled into their heads for owing less.

The hospital said it was lucky she found him when she did, because without treatment he could have ended up wandering the streets and straying out onto the road if he didn't die of exposure first. They didn't know the half of it. The most dangerous thing would have been if he'd wandered back into the less than loving embrace of a steel blade wielded by one of McPhee's crew. One of McPhee's lot was nicknamed 'the surgeon' because his hobby was carving folk new smiles.

There was no time for small talk. "I need a passport," she said.

Donald threw back his head and laughed. "That I can do. I am magic man."

She found that difficult to believe considering the state he and his flat were in. Tragic man, more like.

With nowhere else to go, Kirsty was forced to stay there.

She didn't sleep well, tossing and turning so much she kept herself awake. Her mind was on too many things. Her life had become like an episode of *The Wire*.

When she did get some sleep, she was awoken by a shuffling figure sitting on the one good chair, staring into space.

"It's the zombie invasion," she could remember thinking, before turning to face the other way and going back to sleep.

When she got up, some sunlight was streaking in through the bed sheets haphazardly put up over the windows instead of curtains. Donald had left a note, wanting to meet her at Buchanan Bus Station at 1pm. He must have the passport.

Pulling herself together, she went to the bathroom and splashed some water on her face, wincing when she saw her reflection. She tried to fix it with the little makeup she had with her, the face powder she kept in the pocket of her jeans.

Then she walked out into the cold morning air. A safe deposit box was calling her.

● ● ●

Waiting in Buchanan Bus Station for Donald was a demoralizing experience. Everyone seemed to be either part of a happy group heading off on some trip or another, chatting away and sipping vending machine coffee, whilst bitching away about work colleagues or talking about the telly they watched last night. She envied their simple lives. She was getting ready to flee for her life with the clothes she was standing in, with no idea of what was going to happen to her.

The security man eyed Donald as he sauntered into the bus station, hands stuffed into the pockets of his low hung jeans and dreads flying in the wind. Donald was well used to such a reaction. Even in these the days of mass immigration to Glasgow, there weren't many folk as striking as him: the locals were the color of weak tea with stunted growth. And that was the healthy ones.

Donald was tall and as dark as the night sky, and if it wasn't for the fact his clothes were hanging off him because he'd lost so much weight (a crack diet dented the appetite somewhat), he could have been in a Calvin Klein ad.

He saw Kirsty watching him and a huge grin swept across his face. These days it was not a pretty sight because his teeth resembled toothpicks and there were mouth ulcers. He was the after in a drug poster.

"Did you get it?" she said.

"Yeah, have I ever failed you, sweetheart?" There was that grin again, the one that used to be like slipping into a warm bath. Now it was a window into what Donald could have been.

She didn't tell him that discovering he was a hopeless crack addict felt like a betrayal. He was better than this. She knew he was, but the truth was in his wrecked looks. This might be the last time she saw him. A bad batch, an angry customer, and he was a goner. Drug dealers had a very short life expectancy.

He motioned that they should leave the station. He was being smart, keeping their transaction safe from Big Brother and she appreciated that. Maybe his brain wasn't total fried egg.

They walked over to the bus stop opposite the Royal Concert Hall and well away from any cameras. The shelter was empty and they went inside. She handed him the carrier bag containing a few sandwiches inside to hide the bulk of the eight grand in cash she'd brought Donald and he said something about not needing to count it because he trusted her.

She was watching him shove his hand down the front of his jeans where she assumed he'd stashed the passport, when the screech of brakes made her look up.

Before she could figure out what was happening, two beefy men leapt out of a white transit van and grabbed her. Sandwiched between them, there was no chance of escape.

Why wasn't Donald helping her?

She went to shoot him a desperate gaze. But he was gone. Shoulders hunched, he was already walking away. Bastard had set her up.

As she was bundled into the back of the van and the door slammed shut like a steel trap, all she could think was he'd betrayed her.

The van sped off and she was tossed about the floor. From the front of the van, one of her abductors shouted that McPhee wanted to see her. He made it sound as if it was a cordial invitation and not a kidnapping.

Sixteen

AS SHE WAS THROWN ABOUT the van by every pothole and speed bump, Kirsty knew one thing: she didn't want to die. There were things she wanted to do, pigs needing to feel the weight of her stiletto up their arse. But, as she rolled around the van, she knew it was curtains for her once they got to their destination because she didn't have the gun: she'd hidden it at Donald's. The last thing she wanted was to be caught up in Strathclyde Police's crackdown on guns which sometimes meant metal detectors at the bus station.

Her death wouldn't be quick. McPhee's mongrels took a sadistic pride in their work to send out a message to others: screw with us and we'll use a power drill on your kneecaps.

Fear seeped into her every pore and she was forced to bite her lip to stop blubbering. Fat lot of good tears would do her now.

Besides, she wasn't going to be the pathetic, wee lassie they expected her to be, greeting for her life. No, she was going to fight to the end.

Eyeing the door, she wondered if it could be opened from the inside. There was no handle. On her hands and knees, she crawled towards the door. Using her fingers, she felt along the metal for any gaps. There were none wide enough for her to get her fingers in to try to prise it open.

That was the trouble with kidnap vans: they weren't designed for you to get out and they hadn't bothered to tie her up because they knew she couldn't escape.

She needed to find a weapon. Fast.

There was a spare tire in the back, but no jack. What could she do with that? Try and put it over one of the thugs' heads hoopla style? That'd work.

She had to keep searching. There was a sack beside the wheel arch. Scraping along on all fours as the van went round a corner rally car style; she grabbed the bag and peered inside. It was a blowtorch. Great, as well as being sadistically tortured to death she could do a bit of welding.

A spark of an idea recharged her muddled brain. The hired monkeys were going to get an unwelcome suntan. First she needed to find the gas cylinder. She remembered something thumping against her leg as the van took off. Where was it?

She spotted it nestling beside the wheel arch and scrambled along the floor to reach it.

"Now we're cooking with gas," she laughed, like a demented beggar raking in the bins for the last dregs of booze in bottles.

She adjusted the blowtorch, delighted to find that all she needed to do was press the lock button to get a steady flame without keeping her finger on the button.

Meantime the van was being battered by little stones, making her think they must be in the countryside somewhere. It made sense that McPhee would have her taken somewhere quiet and out of the way, where no one where hear her screams. And see them disposing of her body afterwards.

It was now or never.

She let out the biggest howl she could, the one that had been building up inside her for years, ever since the day she was four and daddy put his hands between her legs and left them there, pushing his fingers inside her and licking them clean afterwards. Over the years, he put worse there than his hands. She hoped the bastard was dead.

The van stopped. The front door shuddered. Heavy footsteps landed on the tarmac. Someone was coming to shut her up.

The door was pulled open with so much force she could hear it swinging, but she couldn't see it because she was in the fetal position with her back to the door, writhing about in apparent agony.

"Period pain," she mumbled, rolling about for good measure as the clatter of heavy footwear on metal got closer. "It hurts so much. I need painkillers." Then she added for good measure, "please" in her best pathetic, wee girl voice.

Not surprisingly, McPhee's errand boy was not the caring type. "If you don't shut the hell up, bitch, I will kick you so hard in the stomach your guts will come out." Then he paused and said, "What the fuck is that smell?"

When she heard him moving around the van, she seized her chance.

Blowtorch in hand, she let him have it full in face. There was a burning smell and he shouted "fuck" as his flesh sizzled. Blindly, he grabbed for her, but she managed to get passed him and was climbing out the van when she heard the door slam again followed by footsteps heading her way.

They were on a dirt track and a forest was ahead. *RUN.*

A fist appeared from nowhere and smacked her squarely on the jaw.

Stunned, she tried to keep her hand on the blowtorch and her feet on the ground. She failed on both counts, ending up on the deck and gazing up at a pair of blue jeans. The blowtorch trundled agonisingly beyond her grasp.

"Fuck, darling, you've got some balls."

She gazed up at the voice. The man was grinning at her through nicotine stained teeth. There was something approaching admiration in his voice. He held out a hand and she stared at it for a moment before she let him help her up.

What was his game?

"Is it true you killed that fucker Gavin Reid?"

She gazed up at him blankly. "Who?"

"Fella you killed at McPhee's club. That was his name."

"I guess I did then." No point denying it considering he already knew. "Was he a pal of yours?"

She already knew the answer, but it was best to check. He might be trying to trick her. He hadn't been that pally so far, abducting her and throwing her in the back of the van and then slugging her one.

Blue Jean's expression darkened. "Fuck no. I hated that bastard. He was shagging my wife when I was inside. Back-stabbing, wee shite."

She eyed him. "What happens now?"

He chuckled. It wasn't a nice laugh. Then his fist slammed into her face.

The power of the blow lifted her off her feet and she staggered backwards, falling right on her backside. Blood gushed from her nose and she thought the bastard had broken it until she put her hand on it and felt there was no break.

"You bastard," she wheezed, struggling to get a breath.

She tried to stand, but it was as though she was on a boat

and it was going from side to side. She fell straight back down again.

He grabbed her by the throat and put his foot on her back, pinning her to the ground.

Kneeling down, he spoke softly into her ear. "Listen, sweetheart and listen damn good. I can't let you go. McPhee might believe you got the better of that dunderheid (he pointed in the direction of the van), but not me as well. Nah. No way. He'll get suspicious. I need to finish this."

Kirsty's lip trembled. Was this really how it ended? Betrayed by the one man she thought she could trust and then buried in the woods?

"Are you going to kill me?" Her voice was clear. She wasn't going to show him she was scared.

If this was the end she wouldn't beg for her life. Kirsty McLeod didn't beg. She was a lion, not a pussy cat.

He put his hands around her throat and squeezed. As she struggled, kicking out with her good leg, lashing out with her arms, he told her to relax, to let herself go. She wanted to tell him to get to fuck, but she couldn't summon up the breath and her vision was beginning to blur.

So, this was how it ended.

Seventeen

KIRSTY WOKE UP in the grips of a scream. It was pitch dark and all she could smell was death and decay. Where was she? Was she dead? If she was she'd expected more.

She tried to move, but something heavy was pinning her down. Even moving a fraction to one side was impossible and she couldn't move her arms; they were trapped like the rest of her. A tear rolled down her face. Had she been buried alive?

She knew she wasn't dead. So, where was she? She strained her ears, trying to pick up some clue. She could hear the squawk of seagulls and another sound she recognized. A mechanical digger and it was heading her way.

She must be on some kind of building site or quarry.

Wherever she was, she was having visions of herself being squashed under a giant truck, or even worse, encased, alive in concrete.

Panic gripped her. She had to warn the driver she was here or be mangled under the truck, her bones splintering like twigs. But, how could she do that?

There was nothing she could do to draw their attention; not even a scream because her throat had dried to sandpaper, and anyway, any noise would surely be lost in the racket of the gulls and the truck.

Then the earth moved and she was tossed up in the air. Daylight stung her eyes as she squinted up at the sky. It was its usual gunmetal grey. She stuck out her tongue to catch the rain that fell; it tasted like heaven.

But, there was little time to marvel at the wonders of the universe, and the beauty of being alive. The truck was coming back. If she stayed where she was she'd be flattened for sure. No one would ever find her. No one would ever know. She'd be the bug someone squashed, unimportant and forgotten. Buried under all the household debris, the same as all the rubbish in what she now realized was a landfill site.

Looking down, she saw that her legs were trapped in a carpet. Blue Jeans must have wrapped her in it so he could dump her as per McPhee's instructions. But, why hadn't he killed her? He'd had the chance and surely wouldn't have messed it up unless he'd wanted to.

With one all mighty pull, she yanked her good leg free of the carpet and hopping on one foot, reached down to pull out her prosthetic leg. The bloody thing was stuck. And the digger was getting closer.

She hauled at it again, but no joy. The leg wouldn't budge. There was no way she could leave it behind. It wasn't like you could buy these things in any corner shop.

There was nothing for it. She needed to attract the attention of the digger, somehow.

Scrambling up onto the top of an old TV set, she waved like a lunatic, shouting at the digger to stop, as if the driver could hear above all the racket his vehicle was making. The truck kept coming towards her and she was going to dive to the side at the last moment, when the miracle happened. The driver stopped.

A bemused head appeared out the cab window. Kirsty could only imagine the absurdity of what he saw: an apparition of a woman with a bloody nose, dressed like a scarecrow with decaying food and crap in her hair, hobbling on one leg like a visitation from some post-apocalyptic universe.

"What the fuck?"

He was saying it again and again as she hobbled over to his truck.

She gave him her best flashbulb smile. "Can you wait to do this bit until I find my false leg?"

He gawped at her and she could tell he thought she was a madwoman. Then his face twitched into something approaching anger.

"Is this some kind of student prank, because I've had enough of you work-shy fuckers. My work's hard enough without you lot coming here and…"

She stopped him mid rant with a glare that would have frozen a sauna.

"Listen, pal. I've had a shitty day. No, not day, week, and now I just want to go home. So, if you don't mind, why don't you get lost and leave me to find my leg?"

He eyed her wearily and when he saw her stump something clicked. His features relaxed. "Okay whatever you say, hen."

Before he drove off, he flung her a flask. "Think you need this more than me girl. It's coffee. Bloody awful coffee, but coffee all the same and it has a wee drop of whisky in it. Look like you could use it."

She mumbled her thanks and with a flash of a gap toothed smile, he was off.

• • •

She was dragging her weary body out of the dump, still picking old food and god knows what else from her hair and wondering what the hell she was going to do next because no taxi was going to pick her up in this state in the backside of nowhere, when Mr. Truck man reappeared.

He rolled down her window and waved her over. "Listen, hen, I don't feel right leaving you here. No like this. Can I give you a lift somewhere? Maybe even take you back to my house and you can get cleaned up?"

She sucked in some air. If this bloke thought she was so hard up she'd go back to his to prostitute herself just to get a lift, he was off his head. Not even if he was her best chance of wheels.

Her reaction brought a worried smile. "Naw, hen. You've got the wrong idea. My missus will be there. She's about your size. Could lend you some gear."

She relaxed. Maybe not all men were after one thing.

He opened the cab door and she jumped in.

Once she was seated and they'd left the dump, he turned to her and held out his hand. "I'm Ken by the way."

"Kirsty," she said in reply.

"So, come on, hen. How did you end up as Stig of the dump? I need to tell this story to my mates."

She simply shook her head. How could a man used to the straightforwardness of shoveling up people's household crap and moving it from one spot to another, possibly understand what had happened to her?

Eighteen

THERE WAS NO SIGN of Donald when she used a welding torch to cut through his door. She retrieved the gun from its hiding place and sat down and waited.

With every minute she waited, she got angrier and angrier thinking about all the things she was going to do to that sell out once he arrived.

An hour later, she heard Donald complaining about the door having a bloody great hole in it. When he sauntered into the living room his eyes became saucers when he saw Kirsty sitting there. He blinked, then beamed.

The silly bugger was going to play the innocent card.

"Kirstee, it's so good to see you," he chirped. "I knew you'd escape."

He ran over to her and tried to pull her towards his skeletal frame, but she pushed him off roughly and he fell.

"No thanks to you, you fucking snake."

She ran at him and kneed him in the balls and started kicking and punching him, her satisfaction growing every time she connected. Once she started, she couldn't stop.

"You set me up you bastard. I trusted you. How could you do that to me? I was defenseless. I had no one."

He was on the ground now curled into a ball and she was kicking the hell out of him. And whilst she was doing it she could see the thug she killed, the octopus who'd started it all. Hear the squish as she'd pulled her heel out of his head. See Jamie as he fell, darkness in his once bright eyes. Hear the creak of the stairs as her father paid her a night-time visit. See that finger in a pickle jar.

And every punch and kick was aimed at the lot of them and what they'd done to her. It felt good. She never wanted to stop. She was in a rhythm now.

Donald's cries snapped her out of it and in that moment she saw him for the weak, junkie bum that he was. Someone to be pitied not hated. He'd sold her out for his next fix. What junkie wouldn't? Nothing personal, would have done it to anyone.

She stopped hitting him and forced herself back onto his skuzzy couch. Her heart was beating out a bongo beat and she could hear it reaching a crescendo in her ears. She wanted it to stop because her head hurt.

Putting her head in her hands, she tried to stop the pounding in her head.

When she finally spoke, her voice sounded as if it was coming from a long way off. "I want to kill you. But you're not worth it. But, I need to know one thing…' Donald stopped crying and peered up at her, his eyes bloodshot. "Why did you do it?"

"Who do you think supplies me with the stuff I sell?" he sniffed. "McPhee does. I owe him big time. He was going to kill me."

Kirsty leapt off the couch and grabbed Donald by the

hair. He did nothing to stop her, just hung there in the air as if she was holding up a doll.

"Kill you," she hissed. "You're doing that alright on your own. Look at you. You're a dead man walking."

"I'm sorry," he said. Maybe he genuinely believed he was. But she didn't have time for this.

"Where my money?"

One look at Donald's face and she knew the cash was already gone – spent on more gear. Just as well she'd had the good sense to take the eight grand fee for Donald and stowed the rest.

As Donald slumped to the floor, whimpering, Kirsty cursed herself for ever trusting a junkie. Their loyalty was to drugs and whoever was supplying them. They didn't have friends: just customers and other dealers.

As she walked down the street back towards the Underground, she eyed the Romanian girls standing in doorways and felt a pang of guilt that she couldn't do anything to help them. Then she told herself she couldn't take on other folk's problems because she had enough of her own. Such as how to get another passport for instance. Donald had been her last shot. Who could she trust now?

A sliver of a thought entered her brain and she managed to grab it before it could slip way beyond her reach. If she couldn't rely on people to help her out of loyalty or friendship, then she should consider people who would do anything for money and there were plenty of them.

She found a phone box that didn't stink of pee and look like someone had used the phone to wipe their backside on and dialed a number. Someone answered and she told them what she wanted. They were reluctant to listen to her proposition at first, until she mentioned the money. Then they were very obliging.

Nineteen

SURVEYING HERSELF in the mirror, Kirsty knew that in this getup she'd be lucky to get any tips working as a barmaid. Her flame hair was dyed jet black and she'd colored her eyebrows and eyelashes to match. Add in the Geisha girl white foundation she was wearing, and bright red lipstick and it was Morticia Adams eat your heart out.

But, at least she resembled the picture on the passport she was carrying; scarily so.

The passport was "borrowed" from an old acquaintance of hers, a hostess who used to work at Jimmy's club. Ailsa had helped Kirsty for the ten grand and not for old time's sake; the girl was a mercenary cow. Maybe that's why they got on so well because she was straightforward. She also happened to be about Kirsty's build and height, which helped. If she'd been an Amazon, Kirsty would have been screwed.

As Kirsty skipped through Glasgow Airport, clutching the *Evening Times*, she fought the urge to read it, again. Their top story was a belter. Jimmy McPhee had been charged with the murder of his nephew Jamie. Somehow he'd managed to get bail (he must have had blackmail photos of the judge) even though all the evidence pointed to him. Police believed he'd killed Jamie because he'd been trying to muscle in on the family business.

There was no mention of the concerned citizen who'd helpfully sent the murder weapon to the police. Kirsty would gratefully waive the Crimestoppers reward put up by no other than Jimmy himself.

Before she headed for the departure lounge, Kirsty made one last phone call on Scottish soil. There was something she needed to check on.

She shoved the coins into the slot, dialed a familiar number and waited. But the phone kept ringing out. She glanced at her watch. Ten past ten. Mrs Torrance was always in at this time so she could listen to Woman's Hour and complain about these modern women wanting to work and have kids. Where was she?

A tightness gripped Kirsty's chest. Something wasn't right. Mrs T was a creature of habit. Her whole life revolved around a timetable.

Abandoning the paper in the bin, Kirsty jogged through the airport and towards the exit.

By the time she was out of the building she was running for the coach link to Glasgow with a sinking sense of dread.

Twenty

WHEN SHE REACHED Mrs Torrance's, Kirsty knew something was wrong.

The radio wasn't on. Mrs T always listened to it as she dashed around the house with her feather duster and can of furniture polish, tutting at what she was hearing. She claimed it helped her to relax.

"Cleanliness is next to godliness," she'd chirp.

If that's what it really took to get into heaven, Kirsty was seriously screwed. Her flat always resembled a hovel - after a party arranged on Facebook.

Pressing her ear to the door, she listened. Not a peep. She was going to jump up and peer in the window, when she heard a faint whimpering, not animal but human.

She took the gun she'd retrieved from her place out of her bag and slowly turned the door handle making sure it made no sound. The door opened easily. Far too easily. Mrs T always kept it locked.

With her heart beating a Samba drum in her head, Kirsty

slunk inside.

The living room was empty and looked untouched, except for the can of furniture polish sitting opened on the table.

Gun raised, Cagney and Lacey style, Kirsty made her way towards the kitchen door. If this was a trap she was going to make sure she caused them a bit of damage before they got her.

When she reached the door, she heard moaning. She threw it open, fully expecting to have to start shooting, but there was only one person in the room.

Mrs T was tied to a chair with a clothes rope wound round her waist to bind her to the chair. Her legs were bound rightly together. She'd been gagged with a pair of her tights, but not tightly enough because she'd managed to work some of it free.

Ugly blue bruises were already beginning to form around the old woman's eyes. By the morning, she'd have two great big shiners. Her chin was badly cut as though someone with a heavy ring had belted her one.

There was desperation in her eyes. When she'd heard Kirsty, a part of her must have thought it was her attacker returning to finish the job.

Kirsty undid the gag. It fell onto the floor and she thought she heard Mrs T say thank you, but she couldn't be sure: the woman's voice was faint.

How long had she sat here like this, terrified and helpless, believing that nobody was going to come to save her? Not with Kirsty heading out of the country.

Leaving the other bonds for a moment, Kirsty rushed over to the sink and got some water. Gently she helped Mrs T to drink, a little sip at a time. Then she used scissors from the drawer to cut the woman free.

Kirsty bit back her anger in an effort to sound calm. "Mrs Torrance. What happened?"

Even as she said the words, she knew how meaningless they were. That bastard McPhee had been here, or at least the thugs he hired to do his bidding had been. They'd been looking for her. Mrs T refused to tell them a thing and this is what they'd done to her. The bastards. Even for McPhee this was a new low battering and old lady.

If Kirsty hadn't come along when she did, the poor woman could have died of hypothermia. The room was chilly and it was still daylight. By night-time it would be deadly cold, hardly safe for an immobilized pensioner. Not that Kirsty was a hero, because this had only happened because of what she had done. Mrs Torrance was an innocent victim in all this.

Kirsty tried to dampen the guilt by reasoning that she hadn't expected McPhee and his thugs to target her friend. Why would she when she'd had no idea they even knew there was a connection? It wasn't as though she had mentioned Mrs Torrance to anyone at work.

She'd never confused the camaraderie that co-workers had with friendship. If people knew stuff about you, they always used it as ammunition against you. Kirsty wasn't dumb enough to fall into that trap.

Through sips of water, Mrs T recounted how two men ("a fat one and a thin one") had turned up at her house late last night. They'd posed as gas men – they'd had the uniforms on, the photo ID's and the clipboards – they'd said there was a gas leak in the area. They needed to check her boiler or the whole street could blow up. She'd noticed that one was wearing blue jeans, but had thought nothing of it. It was late, he'd probably been off duty when he'd been called out.

Once inside, they'd grabbed her and forced her to sit in a chair. When she'd protested, warning them to get the hell out of her house or she'd call the police, one of them punched her in the face. She'd fallen and as she'd lain sprawled on the floor, they'd dragged her into the chair and tied her up.

Then the interrogation began. The fat one demanded to know where Kirsty was. He said if she didn't tell them, he'd get a pair of pliers and pull out her fingernails one by one. There was a crazy glint in his eye. He said he'd seen it done in a movie once. When Mrs T said she didn't know, she was punched again. The blow was so powerful the chair had fallen with her on top of it. They'd had to help her up.

When she'd still insisted she'd no idea where Kirsty was (which was the truth, because Kirsty deliberately hadn't told her), Blue Jeans took the biggest serrated knife from the kitchen drawer and holding it so close to her face that she could see her own reflection, had threatened to "cut her from her forehead to her cheek" if she didn't spill. At that point in her story, Mrs T freely admitted she had soiled herself. She thought she was going to die and said a silent prayer.

Then something had happened that had saved her. Someone knocked on her door and shouted out her name and her attackers fled out the back, warning her that they would be back.

Since then, she'd been stuck in that chair, freezing and terrified and wondering if anyone would find her in time. The bastards hadn't even bothered to untie her.

All Kirsty could think of as she listened to this sorry tale, was McPhee would pay for what he'd done, in a way he did not expect. She was going after him.

It was bad enough that he wanted Kirsty and the cash she'd stolen from him, but to take it out on an old woman. That was despicable.

Just as it had in the club, rage burned up inside her and all sense of reason was incinerated in her blazing fury. Jimmy McPhee was a dead man.

Using the excuse that she was going to call an ambulance, she retreated to the hall where the phone was located and in rapid succession thumped her head off the wall twice. That seemed to calm her.

Mrs T had been to the bathroom and was now draped in a shawl, hugging herself as she sat on the couch, when Kirsty re-entered the room.

She smiled faintly at Kirsty. "I'll be alright, dear."

Kirsty told her the ambulance is on its way.

"There's no need, dear."

Kirsty shook her head. "Best to get you checked out. See if anything is broken."

The old woman nodded. "If you say so."

Kirsty knelt down on the floor beside the couch. "I'm so sorry I brought this to your door Mrs Torrance. I—"

She had to stop talking because her eyes were misting with tears and a lump the size of a grapefruit was forming in her throat.

"I know, dear," said Mrs T. "Whatever trouble you're in, you must tell the police."

Kirsty gave an ironic laugh. "It's gone too far for that." And it had. If the police didn't nail her for the two murders, then McPhee would get her. There was nothing left for her but to run. Get her dog and go.

"Where's Benjy?" said Kirsty. Her calmness was gone, replaced by gripping terror, the kind that grabs you by the throat and won't let go.

There was no sign of him. Had those thugs killed him and stuck him in a cupboard somewhere? If they had, she'd track them down and torture them in ways they couldn't possibly imagine. Anger would make her so bloody creative. She'd paint the walls with their blood and take a garlic press to their cocks and leave them to bleed to death.

Surely even the clowns employed by McPhee would know not to lay a finger on her dog?

Sadistic bastard that he was, McPhee had been gutted when a rival gangster had robbed his bookies and shot dead his Rottweiler. When the shooter was caught, McPhee had personally cut off the man's balls with a rusty pair of garden shears as two of his goons held the man down and grinned underneath their masks.

The story had been treated like an urban myth until someone had posted the video nasty on YouTube: it took the site two hours to take it down and by then there'd been thousands of hits.

At the question, the woman stiffened. "I let the wee girl who lives across the street take him for a walk. I think it was her and her ma at the door that scared those men off."

Kirsty planted a smacker on her cheek and hugged her. The woman smiled and for the first time since she entered the flat, Kirsty grinned back. Behind the smile, she had come to a decision.

There was only one way to end this: with a bullet in McPhee's sorry excuse for brain. And she was the girl to do it.

Twenty-One

NOW THEY WERE TWO FOLK DOWN, Kirsty knew McPhee's would be looking for some bar staff. Who better to fill in than an experienced barmaid such as herself? It would be the last place McPhee would expect to find her.

First she needed a disguise. One good enough to fool McPhee and anyone else who knew her. It was time to go shopping.

Two hours later, Kirsty wanted to puke when she examined herself in the mirror. Gone was her red hair, replaced with a trashy blonde that made her look like the kind of girl who should be pulling punters and not pints. Daisy Duke's hotpants clung to her like a second skin and the tight pink top she wore might as well have been emblazoned with the message "Grab me."

Scrutinizing the new her, she groaned. The sooner this was over the better.

The only thing she was wearing that she did like, were red knee high boots she'd spotted in the window of a designer store. They'd set her back 500 quid, but they'd been worth every penny. She felt like Xenia Warrior Princess in them and would have fancied herself to give anyone a good kicking.

She got a further kick out of the fact that unwittingly McPhee had paid for them.

The boots also doubled up as a great place to stash a gun, as she fully intended to be packing. McPhee wouldn't die as easily as the letch she killed. She needed to do it the old fashioned way. A bullet to the brain and no messing.

Taking a deep breathe, Kirsty handed the taxi driver a fiver and some coins and got out of the cab, planting one boot on the pavement first and gazing down the street before she put the other foot down. If she'd seen anyone she knew, she would have jumped back in that cab and gone somewhere to recheck her disguise and down a few drinks first.

Since she'd hatched this plan, she'd been trying to kid herself that killing McPhee would be easy, but she was dreading what she had to do next and sick with worry.

She felt like crap: a vein in her forehead was throbbing as though an alien was about to burst out of it. The nausea reminded her of that time she'd drank flaming Sambuca until two in the morning at a pal's hen night. The nasty thoughts bouncing round her head like *Grand Theft Auto*: The Glasgow housing scheme version weren't helping either.

What if the bastard still recognized her? What the hell then? She was no longer afraid of dying. The dying would be the least painful thing; the torture first would be the real bitch.

Kill McPhee? There was more chance of her giving herself a third eye.

Pushing those thoughts to the back of her mind where they belonged – she needed to do this - she strode up to the club, hiding her trepidation behind her swagger. She rapped three times on the door.

"It's open," a female voice shouted.

With a trembling hand, she turned the handle on the door and it opened with its usual creak, which brought a quick smile to her face. Lazy bastards still hadn't bothered to oil the thing.

Head up and shoulders back, she strutted into the club. When she realized who was there, she wanted to walk straight back out again.

A tough old bird in her late 50's, with grey hair everyone knew she dyed black, bar manager Angie was supposed to be on holiday in Gran Canaria. Kirsty almost asked how her holiday went, but managed to bite her lip just in time. Rumbled the first time she opened her gob? That wasn't happening.

"Can I help you love?" Angie spoke in a Cockney twang, still present despite the twenty odd years she'd spent in Glasgow looking after McPhee's club.

Kirsty had never been fooled by that friendly façade. She knew everybody's mate Angie, was McPhee's spy in this place and wouldn't hesitate to drop one of her staff if it were in her best interests to do so, not to mention play deaf and dumb when it suited her. She hadn't even bothered to try and contact Melissa when she hadn't shown up for work. Maybe, because she'd known about Jamie's sideline into murder. Or perhaps because she simply didn't give a shit.

Angie would have gone mental when she'd found out about the guy Kirsty had banjoed. Not out of any concern for one of McPhee's grunts, but because her usually pristine floor would need a good scrub.

Kirsty put on her best smile; one that brought out the dimples on her cheeks and made her want to gag. Who wanted to look like Shirley bloody Temple in Glasgow?

"I'm looking for some bar work. I have lots of experience."

Kirsty was pleased with how her voice sounded; those over-lays for her teeth had transformed her voice.

Angie frowned and it wasn't a pretty sight. Her sixty-a-day fag habit and tanning booth obsession meant she was as wrinkly as a pensioner's after a long bath. A frown made a crater appear in her forehead.

Angie sucked in her lips. "Don't I know you from somewhere?"

The adrenaline that'd been cruising through Kirsty's veins turned to dread. Had she been rumbled? Surely, if Angie had rumbled her she'd have made some excuse and disappeared round back to phone Jimmy or one of his rent-a-thugs? Or just have gone for the baseball bat Kirsty knew she kept behind the bar.

Kirsty straightened up. It was time to start playing the part.

Flashing a wee smile, she shook her head enough to make the trashy chain belt around her waist jingle. "Nah, I've just moved to Glasgow. Me and my wee girl Chantelle Tinker-belle. She's only three and she did the cutest thing the other day. She..."

Kirsty hated the dumb girl voice she'd put on. But, needs must and all that. She needed to become the single mum who'd been left on the shelf, but who was still trying to find a man who didn't say he was nipping out to buy a packet of fags and not come back.

She was relieved when Angie butted in, because thinking up an amusing anecdote on the spot about a daughter she didn't even have, would have been tricky.

"We might need some bar staff," said Angie, finger-ing those ugly lampshade sized earrings she always wore. "Call round tomorrow night and I'll see what I can do." An exasperated smile flashed across her lips and she made a sweeping movement with her arms. "It's the boss's birthday, and it'll be a bit manic or I'd give you a start tonight."

The usually all seeing all telling Angie didn't notice the little leap Kirsty made. So it was McPhee's birthday. She'd definitely have a wee keepsake for him. A wee memento to remember her by. If she could get in.

It was time to push it. She'd never have a better time to have a go at McPhee than at a party. He wouldn't be expecting it. Not in his palace as he called the club. And neither would his hired muscle. They'd been too busy getting steaming and ogling the strippers.

"I'm sure I could handle it tonight," Kirsty said, with a wee smile of her own. "If you need the help? I've done parties at all sorts of places, including lap-dancing clubs. I know the drill."

Angie eyed the clock above the bar. "I'm sure we can cope. I'm way ahead of schedule. The stripper's booked and the cake. But, ta anyway. Come back tomorrow."

Damn. What now? Tomorrow would be too late.

Then she thought about the stripper and she relaxed. "Okay, thanks. I'll be back then."

And with a wee skip, she was out of there not even bothering that a delivery driver tried to slap her on the backside as she passed him outside the club. Usually she'd have kicked him in the balls.

Who said she needed anger management classes? She was in perfect control of her emotions.

Twenty-Two

A FEW HOURS LATER, Kirsty was sitting in the Bus Stop café, trying to avoid the sludge passing for tea and eating a roll made with cheese so plastic she had to fight the temptation to throw it against the peeling wall to see if it would bounce. It was just as well she wasn't there for the quality of the food or the ambience. This place scored nil point on both scores.

It was the quality of the vantage point that had attracted her. From here she could see the back entrance of the club in all its sleazy glory. So far, she'd witnessed a tramp taking a dump in one of the bins and a baseball capped figure handing in a box to someone at the back door.

There were no signs of the stripper, but she was pretty sure she'd be along soon. There's no way Angie would risk the girl going through the bear pit of the bar. Poor girl would never make it out alive. That's why Angie always got the entertainment to report to the back entrance.

Kirsty had been gazing out the window for an hour and 44 minutes (she'd counted every minute) and was so bored out of her skull, she'd been reduced to playing a game of let's pretend. She'd made it fun by imagining all manners of ways of killing McPhee.

So far, she'd vaulted over the bar, gun raised and shot him dead in one slick movement. The drink he'd held had clattered to the floor, merging with his blood as all around people screamed.

In another, she'd waited for him in the toilet he reserved for personal use and emerged from behind the shower curtain *Psycho* style. Only instead of a knife she had a gun. She'd aimed and shot him in the chest. He'd keeled over with his trousers down around his ankles and a look of complete astonishment on his face.

Her personal favorite was where he demanded to be left alone with her in his office for his "birthday present." When it was just the two of them, she pulled out the gun and ordered him to kneel on all fours and lick her boots. Once he'd done that to her satisfaction, she'd told him he could live. As relief washed over his hideous face, she'd shot him in the head. A red splotch appeared on his forehead and he'd tumbled to the floor. As he lay there, she'd given him one last kick with her boot to make sure he was dead. That's when he groaned and she'd pumped two bullets into his chest.

But dreams were one thing, reality was another. Could she really go through with it? She wasn't *La Femme Nikita*.

She was just thinking that when she spotted the stripper. A tall blonde in fishnets and a nearly there skirt, the girl was so much of a stereotype it wasn't true. Kirsty almost wanted to run over and give her fashion tips. Like put on a skirt that at least covers your knickers. Those girls put it all on show, they didn't know how to tease and tantalize.

Kirsty rushed out of the café and across the street. There was time for her to make it before the girl worked out that she needed to buzz the security entrance and wait patiently until someone could be bothered to answer it.

The girl must have heard her coming because she turned round. 'Do you work here?" she asked Kirsty. "Maybe you can let me in."

Kirsty grabbed her arm. "Listen love, the agency screwed up. This is my gig."

The girl scowled. It put ten years on her. "Who says so?" She stiffened up and gave Kirsty the once over the way women did.

Kirsty glared at her. "I do. Now why don't you just fuck off? The job's taken."

She released the girl's arm fully expecting her to scuttle off. Instead Blondie ignored her and began rummaging through her bag. "The agency. I'm going to call them. You can't do this."

Before she could do any more searching, Kirsty caught her full handed with a slap across her face. The girl let out a squeal and fell backwards. The contents of her bag scattered onto the cobbles. Tampons, keys, lipstick and spare change littered the pavement. Kirsty scooted down to pick them up as the girl glared at her like a surly school kid.

Kirsty stood up. "If you don't want to get hurt, you'd better get going."

She held out a hand.

The girl ignored it (probably because she was wary of the mad cow who'd just belted her one) and pulled herself to her feet. A tear trickled down her cheek, smudging her blusher and she brushed it quickly away.

"What did you do that for?" Her lips trembled when she spoke, but she still tried to look hard with a stance more suited to a bouncer than a stripper. The tough girl act was fooling no one.

A trace of a smile played on Kirsty's lips. She admired the girl's balls. If someone had done that to her years ago, she'd have scrammed, no questions asked.

But this wasn't the time for sentiment. Life was tough shit. Let the girl learn that early and have time to toughen up before she ended up swimming in the Clyde, in a sack tied with a brick.

Hand on hips, Kirsty stare leached onto the girl until she looked away. "If you don't leave now, I'm going to rearrange your face. Got it?"

The girl meekly nodded. Then she turned and sullenly walked back the she'd come, tottering on her heels, her handbag swinging in time to her walk, mumbling away no doubt about the psycho bitch.

Kirsty watched her go, with a shitty feeling she wasn't used to; maybe because she wasn't used to hitting wee lassies. The girl hadn't done anything to her, yet she'd belted her and now she was stealing her gig. For all she knew the girl could have two kids to feed at home, and a mean bastard for a boyfriend who'd knock her into next week for not making enough money.

Against her better judgment Kirsty shouted the girl back, asked her how much she was being paid and then gave her double.

"Look," she said, before the girl had left, glowering at her good style, "you may not realize it, but I'm doing you a big favor. The punter's a slimy toad. The kind of slime that doesn't wash off."

With one last glower, the girl was gone.

Kirsty pressed the buzzer. There was no answer, so she waited a few minutes and pressed it again. Sometimes it was too noisy in the club for anyone to hear, but at least there was no danger of Angie answering – in the two years that Kirsty had worked there, not once had the woman answered the door. No, she left that to her flunkies.

Angie's position as Queen Bee, puzzled Kirsty. Why did McPhee trust her so much? She wasn't family and it wasn't like he was jumping her bones: Angie was in her 50's, which was about 40 years older than the girls he usually went for. And she wasn't in a school uniform.

After a few minutes she heard a male voice. "Aye. Who is it?"

"My name's Kylie. The agency sent me." Kirsty had seen the name on the girl's credit card when she'd scooped to pick up her stuff.

There was a clunk as she was buzzed in. This is it, she thought, as the sound of her boots hitting the floor reverberated down the short corridor. Showtime.

She'd made it past the utility cupboards when a booming voice called out to her. "Aye, there you are. About bloody time. Thought I was gonna have to do it myself."

When she came face to face with the speaker, she had to dig a nail into her palm to stop herself from laughing. McPhee would have had a hairy canary if the flabby, sweaty bastard before her started gyrating to music and taking his egg stained jumper off to reveal his man boobs.

With one podgy paw, he motioned for her to follow him into a room where the "hostesses" who worked in the club must have come to get a break from the handsie punters.

Once she'd followed the waddling figure inside, he said nothing whilst his weaselly eyes roamed her body. Instantly she wanted to jump in a bath of Carbolic.

What was he doing – looking for a bloody hallmark? Screw this. She'd only met the man and already she wanted to teach him a lesson in manners, preferably with a well aimed kick at his wobbly gut. Would it sound like a deflating balloon when she connected? Maybe she should put it to the test?

She managed to pull herself back just in time. If she battered Fat Man she'd attract some unwanted attention before she could get a chance to execute her plan.

Finally, he licked his slug lips and signed. "You're a bit long in the tooth to be doing this, darling. Maybe I should phone the agency to get a replacement. Mr. McPhee will no be a happy bunny."

Cheeky bastard.

Again, Kirsty fought the overwhelming urge to kick him in the balls, but resisted. There wasn't the time. So, she did something she never did: she buttoned her lip.

He reached into a corner of the room and produced a sparkly bra and thong and threw it towards her, a big smirk on his face that made her want to slap it off. "Put these on."

She caught them. The silver thong was small enough to floss her teeth and if the sorry excuse for a bra had been just a teensy bit bigger it would have doubled as nipple tassels. This had to be some kind of windup.

Even strippers wore clothes, right? The world was a messed up place, but not so screwed up that that had changed.

She rolled her eyes. "Where's the other gear I've to wear?"

He grinned, exposing matchsticks instead of teeth. "That's it, sweetheart."

Maybe it was his attitude she couldn't stomach, or him calling her sweetheart. Or the fact that there was no way she could hide the gun or her prosthetic leg in that getup. Whatever the reason, she couldn't rein it in any longer.

"You are fucking kidding."

Fists clenched, she marched up to him and thrust the offending garments under his nose, resisting the urge to twang his beak with the bra strap. His smirk changed into a sneer.

"Listen," she told him, "If you want me to do this job, you better give me some real clothes to wear."

He moistened his lips with his tongue. Yuck, they resembled snail trails. "Stop taking the piss, doll and put on the gear. They're bringing the cake out in fifteen minutes. You need to get ready to jump out of it."

What cake? Nobody had mentioned a cake.

Shite. This latest development scuppered her plans. She'd been all geared up to come to this shit-hole, perform a wee dance and offer McPhee something more if he took her back to his office. Then when his mind was on other things, she was gonna shoot the bastard in the head after she forced him to kneel.

She hadn't planned for anything else: like jumping out of a cake.

How did you do that anyway – eat your way out? Or was it some magic trick?

She eyed Fat Man like he was an out-and-out nutjob and he immediately took offence.

His face flushed with anger. "You do know how to do this, don't you? The agency told me you'd done it before. Said it was a specialty of yours." His round, fat head was starting to get very red, and she was pretty sure if she kept watching it steam would start to appear.

Grinning away at the thought of McPhee's face when she jumped out of his cake and instead of giving him a wee show, blew his brains out, she nodded. "Aye, I've done it before. No worries. Piece a cake."

He didn't laugh at he wee joke.

Kirsty pointed at the bag over her shoulder. "I'll do it, but I choose what to wear."

Maybe this cake lark would work out better? Give her a better chance of escape.

She was too busy thinking it over, plotting how to get away that she thought she'd misheard him at first when he told her to take her clothes off.

She gave him her best what did you say stare and the stupid bastard didn't flinch. He would have if he'd known she'd already killed two men and was planning to kill a third. If he didn't stop being such a pervy bastard, there was a red dot on his forehead.

He repeated what he'd said, telling her he needed to see her with the gear on.

She could imagine him saying that to other girls and them meekly complying, tears stinging their eyes from the humiliation, their tough girl act dissolving because they didn't want to be the girl with the bad attitude. The stroppy cow that didn't get the gigs.

Maybe she could save a bullet for him. She had a pretty good idea where it would go.

"No chance," she told him, her face impassive.

If this has been normal circumstances, before she killed and went on the run with McPhee's cash and shooter, she would have simply walked towards him as though she was going to do what he said and stick the head in him. But, she needed this flunkies' help if she was going to pull this off. That meant behaving as a stripper would and not the psycho bitch she really was.

"I'll put my gear on, but not while you're watching. And...' She pointed down at her boots. "These boots stay on."

He advanced towards her. Big, bloody mistake.

Throwing her hair back from her face, she snarled. "Come any closer and you'll get a tattoo of my boot up your arse." She swung a boot in his direction to demonstrate.

He took a telling and with a tired sigh, waddled out of the room, shouting after him that she had five minutes to get ready and he'd be coming for her.

Not that Kirsty needed any encouragement. If McPhee wanted someone to jump out of his birthday cake, then that was what she was going to do with bells on.

Twenty-Three

SAFELY CONCEALED INSIDE the cake, Kirsty was amazed at how big the prop was. She'd had visions of having to kneel down inside, wound tightly into a tiny ball, fighting claustrophobia and maybe even having to eat her way out, but the reality was different. There was more than enough space for her. The cake was three tiers, wedding cake style, except it wasn't a real cake. The icing on the outside may have been real (it certainly smelt real), but that the rest of it was made out of heavy duty cardboard and completely hollow inside.

Getting inside the cake had been a doddle. A side section came away and all she had to do was walk in and the section was shut behind her. She'd been informed by creepy Colin (he'd been all chummy when he'd came back for her) to jump out on the third "Happy birthday" of the chorus of the Stevie Wonder song they were playing and "Waggle her tits about." He'd said it with a slimy grin and yet again she'd managed to resist the temptation to cave in his thick, ugly skull.

Once she'd climbed inside the cake, she'd given the section

a wee shove and been delighted when it opened outwards easily. The last thing she needed was for it to get stuck, trapping her inside. She'd have coped with having to clamber out the top but she'd prefer not to. Not in these boots and carrying a gun. That would have delayed her escape if she didn't trip over and blow her own damned head off first. As hell bent on revenge as she was, she had every intention of getting the hell out of here once she'd killed that bastard.

The band was playing Superstition when the cake was wheeled into the room. All around her Kirsty could hear people chatting away and their hoots of booze fuelled, too loud laughter.

Let them laugh now, they wouldn't be doing it when she took McPhee's head off.

Reaching down into her boot, she felt the reassuring weight of the fully loaded gun. In her other boot she'd brought something else with her: a CS gas canister. Any numpty dumb enough to come near her, was getting it full in the face.

When the band started playing Happy Birthday to you, her body tensed as she stood up, readying herself to make her big entrance. Part of her was a nervous wreck. Could she really do this? But there was another part of her that was relieved: tonight she was gonna finish this once and for all.

When her cue came, she rose into the air and as the people in the room shrieked with delight, she came face to face with Jimmy McPhee. There was a genuine look of surprise on his face and not because he recognized her either; he seemed amazed that a woman was coming out of his cake. In his blootered state he must have thought the cake was real.

Kirsty smiled at him, the first genuine smile she'd had in a long time and held up the gun. It was fully loaded. She was a regular Annie Oakley now - she'd ditched the empty casings in the Clyde and reloaded (it was amazing what you could find out on the Internet).

She raised the gun, and even as she did so there was still that look of almost child-like wonder on McPhee's face. He had not been expecting this.

Somewhere in the room someone screamed. They knew what was coming before Jimmy did.

Kirsty didn't realize that she'd fired until she saw the Hindu style red dot appear on McPhee's forehead. One of his grunts had been standing by his side and had been about to shove his boss out the way when Kirsty fired. With a start, she realized it was the same guy who'd near choked her and dumped her in the landfill site. He was still wearing blue Jeans.

McPhee hung there for a moment, a puppet being held up by its strings. A look of surprise spread across his face.

He yelled. "Ma, fucking cake. You've ruined ma cake."

As he fell, one hand reached out wildly to grab her but missed.

Then it was pandemonium as everyone ducked, convinced the mad assassin was going to spray the room with bullets. Kirsty got out of the cake and fled out the same entrance she'd been wheeled in just minutes before.

No one followed her as the sound of her heart pounded in her ears. She felt exhilarated: the way she had after a parachute jump. She couldn't believe what she'd just done. McPhee wouldn't be coming after her now. He wouldn't be going after anyone.

As she ran out the back entrance and into the alleyway where she'd left a change of clothes in one of the bins, she was amazed no one was barring her way. This was too easy she thought as she threw on jeans and jumper.

She'd just pulled on the clothes when a hand appeared

from nowhere and grabbed her by the shoulder. Unexpected as it was, she managed not to make a sound.

"Hello Kirsty, it's been a long time sweetheart."

Kirsty's elation turned to dread. She knew that voice; too well.

She turned around to confirm her worst fears.

"Come on sweetheart, have you no got a hug for your old da?"

As always his breath reeked of booze and fags.

Twenty-Four

KIRSTY HAD NO CHOICE but to get in the clapped out Ford Cortina with her old man after he made it clear he'd seen her kill McPhee. He'd have marched her back into the club otherwise. Tam McLeod's only loyalty was to whoever was paying for his next pint and bookies line. Certainly not to the family he'd buggered off on two decades before, after saying he was nipping out to buy some fags.

Although she hadn't realized it until years later, that had been the best day of Kirsty's life. No more nightly visits. By then she was 11 and knew what he did was wrong and didn't make her "special."

Refusing to let him see her shock, she sat there defiantly with her chin jutting out; a pose that would have got her a smack in the jaw when she was a kid. Let him try that now and she'd tear him a new hole. The gun was back in her pocket.

He was too busy swigging from the bottle of Jack Daniels he kept under the driver's seat to notice the loathing in her eyes.

Some things never changed. Once an alchy, always an alchy.

"How did you know I'd be here?" she asked him. *What was his game?*

As manky as ever, he brushed his hand across his nose to wipe away the snot as he drove. "Jimmy and me go way back. You know that. He invited me to this shindig. No doubt wanting to show off as usual. Flash bastard. Glad he's deid."

Dread burrowed its way into her insides like a tapeworm. He knew what she'd done. What now? She'd been fired up before, but now all she felt was fear; the kind that waits to pounce out of the shadows of a dark alleyway as you try to get away from the maniac. Tam McLeod always managed to drain every last ounce of confidence out of her.

He kept on talking, and although she heard the words none of them registered. He could have been talking Swahili for all she knew instead of his usual shite.

"Wow, you really gave it to him, sweetheart. Never thought you had it in you. Always thought you was a gobby wee cow, you were always mouthing off to me, but a punch in the jaw certainly shut you up."

His laugh set her teeth on edge. He'd laughed the first time he raped her like it was some big joke. Sick bastard.

He was weaving up and down the road now, trying to avoid all the parked cars. Not easy to do when he was driving like it was the Gumball Rally. He was too pie-eyed to realize it was his car that was swaying and swerving, not the world.

She needed to get out of this car before the police stopped them or the stupid bastard killed them both. The police would think they'd hit the jackpot with a murderer in the car still carrying the weapon. They'd see it as an open and shut case when they should have been giving her a medal for ridding the city of scum.

He was talking about her mother now, asking her how

she was and Kirsty wanted to grab him by the throat and spit in his face. How could he not know that his own wife had died of cancer? A disease Kirsty believed was brought on by the miserable existence she'd endured as the wife of the piece of crap sitting across from her acting as if this was some happy family reunion, when the truth was his own daughter despised him as much as she'd despised herself whenever he'd laid his filthy paws on her and she'd known it was wrong but could do nothing to stop it.

How could she tell anyone about what he did? They'd just call her a whore and a tease, like he had.

"Don't tell or I'll hurt your ma." That was his mantra every Friday he let her mum go to the bingo so he could be alone with his young daughter.

But, she wasn't that wee frightened lassie anymore and her mum wasn't around for him to hurt.

She pulled the nib up on the passenger door and heard the reassuring click as the lock disengaged. There wasn't just a click in the door, there was a click in her brain.

"You can let me off here," she said firmly, gaze on the door. Even the mere sight of him made her want to vomit.

He glanced over at her, disappointment behind those bloodshot eyes. "What do you mean? You've only just met up with your old man. Why would you want to leave so soon?"

Because you're a dirty bastard, she wanted to say. The kind of pervert who fiddles with his own wee girl. Tells her it's to make daddy happy. Then when she starts to think that maybe he's right, that her daddy loves her more than anyone in the whole world, he ups sticks and buggers off to jump on the bones of another wee lassie and another after that.

She didn't have to know where he'd been to know that she wouldn't have been his only victim. There were more: she knew it in her gut.

It took her years of therapy to realize the abuse wasn't her fault. Her dad was a pedophile, the kind who should be strung up and castrated with a rusty razor blade by the mothers of the kids he abused.

He put his hand on her arm and she pulled it away as if he'd burnt her with his lighter.

"Don't be like that, sweetheart," he said brightly. "This is a happy reunion. Don't you have a kiss for your dad?"

Anger welled up inside her, making her whole body shake with rage. The kind of all consuming rage that had been building up for years only to be unleashed in McPhee's club on that pig who'd kicked the whole thing off with his wandering paws, trying to get inside her knickers. Not taking no for an answer.

"Listen, da," said Kirsty. The word da was uttered with a sneer. There was an expression on his face she'd never seen before: fear. "You're a kiddie fiddling, drunken bastard and I want no more to do with you. If you don't let me out of this car I will take this gun…" She pulled it out of its hiding place. "…and shoot you in the crotch. Got it?"

His bottle of Jack Daniels fell to the floor with a crash and a skinny hand, nails yellowed by years of the fags, tried to grab her. Her reaction was swift. She shoved the butt of the gun in his face.

The car swerved and came to an abrupt stop a few feet away from a lamppost. His head slammed against the windscreen with a thud, and he thumped backwards into the seat, his hand gripping her arm. The guy was a human limpet.

The gaze that used to bore into her skull when he looked down at her, was replaced by a dazed expression and she realized she was no longer scared of him. There was nothing left for her to fear. He was nothing but a worthless, jakey bum.

Her lips curled at the edges. What a night this had been.

"I've killed three men already," she told him calmly; not boasting, just telling it like it was. "…and I won't think twice about shooting you in the head as well. Now I'm going to get out and unless you want to be driving with three eyes instead of two, you will never lay another finger on me."

He let go and that's when she saw it in his eyes: a window into the past where he'd abused her every chance he got, a future where he'd grass her up for the price of a pint.

And what had he done once he'd no longer had access to her? She knew he was a pedophile and perverts didn't stop fiddling with kids. They just moved on to new prey. Only she could save any other kids from the beast.

"Is that your betting line on the floor?" She pointed in the direction of a piece of paper lying on the well worn carpet.

As he bent down to retrieve it, she raised the gun to the back of his skull and fired. In the confined space of the car, the sound was deafening, reminding Kirsty of the time she'd stood too close to a firework. The whole car shook.

A glob of flesh splattered against the driver's window and she watched it with wonder, casually brushing off some of the brain mince that landed on her cheek as if it were a speck of dirt and not a piece of a human being. The sour stench of pish and something worse filled the car. Kirsty never knew that death could smell so bad.

With one last look to make sure the bastard was really dead she opened the car door and jumped out. As she ran, part of her still couldn't quite believe that he was dead. It seemed too easy: maybe she'd thought he'd dissolve into pieces like a TV demon. But real monsters never did.

They were flesh and blood.

Twenty-Five

KIRSTY TWIRLED THE LITTLE UMBRELLA that came with the sunshine cocktail that had a name she couldn't remember, and took a dainty sip. She was reclining on a sun lounger, wearing a bikini that caressed her curves, and fully enjoying being waited on by a hunky waiter. Things could not get any better than this.

Mrs Torrance was sitting there beside her, with a wide brimmed hat and movie star shaded to protect her from the Portuguese sun. Since they'd arrived, she hadn't stopped singing the Algarve's praises. Not bad for a woman who had vowed never to leave Scotland. Not a big fan of "foreign food," apparently. After all, she'd been through it was good to see her relax.

Somewhere in a nearby pool, Benjy was enjoying a dip. Dogs weren't usually allowed on the resort, but it was amazing what a little money could do. Throw it at people and they were liable to have their minds changed about almost anything. Benjy even stayed in their hotel room. Mrs Torrance was still a bit wary of being left on her own, which suited Kirsty. She enjoyed the company and having someone mother her for a change.

After all that had gone on, leaving Scotland had been easy. Despite Kirsty's fears, they'd been no trouble with her passport. They'd barely glanced at it.

The papers were saying that Jimmy McPhee had been the victim of a gangland hit. Witnesses claimed he'd been taken out by a hit man dressed as a woman who jumped out of his birthday cake. Well, it wasn't like Jimmy's lot could admit he'd been offed by a barmaid with one leg, dressed as a stripper? Even dead, McPhee had a reputation to uphold.

The word was Nan had taken over his empire. Give it a few weeks of her running the show, and his thugs would want to resurrect their old boss so they could rid themselves of the crazy cow.

Going back to her hotel room to change into someone nice for dinner, she was alarmed to see that there was a key card in the room door. Maybe it was housekeeping in to change the sheets?

Putting her ear to the door, she listened. Someone was going through the drawers. She could hear them being slammed opened and things being thrown around the room. An opportunistic thief perhaps? Aye, and Jerry Lee Lewis genuinely had great balls of fire.

Taking the gun she'd bought from a dealer when she'd arrived in Portugal (she'd been loathe to part with her old, trusted friend, but had seen no way to get the revolver passed security), Kirsty slowly opened the door and with the barrel leading the way crept into the room.

She almost yelled when she saw who was there.

It was Gregor, as big and ugly as ever. But it couldn't be him: Gregor was dead. There had to be two of them. Twins.

It was the only possibly explanation. Kirsty remembered every inch of the face that had manically tortured her with that knife. Either it was his twin or he had a doppelganger. He'd definitely been dead when she'd taken the gun.

"Hello Gregor Mark 2," she said, pointing the gun at him.

She might as well have been pointing a pea shooter for all the reaction she got. Maybe it just took so long for a fact to register in that pea sized brain of his. Or perhaps he genuinely thought he could hold out his hand and deflect a bullet superhero style.

Whatever the reason, Gregor II stood there a human statue, gazing at her through stone eyes. The huge knife he'd be holding fell with a soft thud onto the carpet.

She raised the gun, preparing to fire when he began to show signs of life.

He held out both palms, telling her not to fire.

An unfamiliar emotion stopped her from firing and she lowered the gun. "Alright," she said, "I won't kill you. One family member's enough." And, she didn't want to start a body trail in Portugal. That's what would get her caught.

She ordered him to empty his pockets. Last thing she wanted was him to phone Nan McPhee. There was a chance that would not end well for Kirsty. Apart from a photo of Kirsty that she couldn't remember being taken, there was some money in his pocket and nothing else.

With her gun still trained on him, she scanned the room. Where could she put him? Then she remembered the closet.

She pointed towards the big walk in closet with the handy lock. It was full of the new clothes she had bought for her new life, but sacrifices needed to be made. She couldn't wear designer gear if she was dead. And she would be if she let the man go.

She motioned for him to step inside. He was uncertain at

first until she raised the gun and pointed it at his huge forehead. Smarter than his brother, he complied. Once he was inside, she turned the key in the lock and moved the heavy marble coffee table over so it was blocking the closet door. Then she put a "Do Not Disturb" sign on the door and left.

She found Mrs T lying in the same spot she'd been in all morning. She was chatting to a young dark-skinned waiter who smiled at her every word.

Kirsty told her they had to leave, now.

Mrs Torrance was genuinely puzzled. "We've only just got here dear. I have things arranged. A massage after lunch with a rather nice young man, and a trip to a local art gallery. Then I thought we could…"

She rambled on about all the things she had planned, but Kirsty wasn't listening. She was too busy phoning the dog sitter, telling him to bring him here pronto.

The call was finished and Mrs T was still nattering away. Something about an art class, or was it pottery? Kirsty grabbed her by the shoulders. She didn't like doing it, but they needed to leave quickly before Nan sent someone else.

"Jimmy McPhee's wife is onto us. One of her thugs was in our hotel room. I locked him in the wardrobe. Nan wants blood. My blood. Either that or me to have her baby. Either way, no ball."

Still no reaction. Kirsty might as well have been pointing out a cloud.

"If you want, you can stay here," Kirsty said gently. She couldn't expect an old woman to run with her. "She doesn't know who you're here. You'll be safe. I'll leave you money. Book yourself into another hotel."

That shook the older woman out of her own wee world. Her eyes focused on Kirsty for the first time and the earnest look made Kirsty smile. "I rather think we should stick together dear." Then with a flash of a smile, "my life was so much duller before you came along."

"Let's go," said Kirsty, grabbing her beach bag.

Her companion packed up her things and followed, not even asking where they were going, which was just as well because for once Kirsty didn't have a plan.

Award-winning Scottish crime writer **JENNIFER LEE THOMSON** who also writes as Jenny Thomson lives in Scotland with her rescue dog and partner and is a member of the UK's Crime Writers Association. She's had a variety of jobs including as a film extra and a board game inventor, and she also worked as a hospital laundry attendant where she narrowly avoided cut off her hand with a stray scalpel left in a doctor's white coat.

Her published works include the dark Scottish crime thriller *Vile City* (featuring Inspector Duncan Waddell), book 2 in the series, *Cannibal City*, will be out soon.

Writing about tough women, she also wrote the crime files trilogy *Hell To Pay*, *Throwaways* and *Don't Come For Me* (featuring rape survivor Nancy Kerr). She used her zombie obsession to write comedy thriller *Dead Bastards*.

She blogs at http://ramblingsofafrustratedcrimewriter. blogspot.co.uk and tweets as jenthom72

BOOKS

On the following pages are a few
more great titles from the
Down & Out Books publishing family.

For a complete list of books and to
sign up for our newsletter,
go to **DownAndOutBooks.com**.

Wear Your Home Like A Scar
Nik Korpon

Down & Out Books
May 2019
978-1-948235-82-2

A clandestine surgeon goes to extreme lengths when she's torn between family loyalties. A con man tries to help his girlfriend escape her pimp, despite what the tarot cards tell her. A drifter hunts down the man who hung her out to dry with a cartel boss. A sicario has a crisis of faith when an old legend stalks him.

From the streets of Baltimore to the comunas of Medellín, the Mexican Sierras to Texas border towns, *Wear Your Home Like a Scar* shows that no matter how deep you cut, you'll never truly leave your home behind.

Murder-A-Go-Go's
Crime Fiction Inspired by the Music of The Go-Go's
Edited by Holly West

Down & Out Books
March 2019
978-1-948235-62-4

The Go-Go's made music on their own terms and gave voice to a generation caught between the bra-burning irreverence of the seventies and the me-first decadence of the eighties.

With a foreword by Go-Go's co-founder Jane Wiedlin and original stories by twenty-five kick-ass authors, editor Holly West has put together an all-star crime fiction anthology.

Main Bad Guy
A Love & Bullets Hookup
Nick Kolakowski

Shotgun Honey, an imprint of
Down & Out Books
978-1-948235-70-9

Bill and Fiona, the lovable anti-heroes of the "Love & Bullets" trilogy, find themselves in the toughest of tough spots: badly wounded, hunted by cops and goons, and desperately in need of a drink (or five).

After a round-the-world tour of spectacular criminality, they're back in New York. Locked in a panic room on the top floor of a skyscraper, surrounded by pretty much everyone in three zip codes who wants to kill them, they'll need to figure out how to stay upright and breathing... and maybe deal out a little payback in the process.

Gravy Train
Tess Makovesky

All Due Respect, an imprint of
Down & Out Books
978-1-64396-006-7

When barmaid Sandra wins eighty grand on a betting scam she thinks she's got it made. But she's reckoned without an assortment of losers and criminals, including a mugger, a car thief and even her own step-uncle George.

As they hurtle towards a frantic showdown by the local canal, will Sandra see her ill-gotten gains again? Or will her precious gravy train come shuddering to a halt?

25083763R10092

Printed in Great Britain
by Amazon

No Borders

A Brampton Poets' Anthology

First Edition: *No Borders, A Brampton Poets' Anthology*

ISBN: 978 1 9173650 1 7

Cover photograph copyright John Langley, of the northern lights on the evening of Friday 10th May 2024 over Brampton.

Cover design Phil Hewitson.

Images freely available in the public domain (p.5, 7, 37, 76, 81, 103).

Photographs copyright of Matthew Taylor (opposite, p.24, 29, 158), John Langley (p.8, 153), Ena Hutchinson (p.13, 14), Kat van Hookens (p.65, 66, 67, 69, 70), Katie Evans (p.84, 85, 87, 88), Stephen Palmer (p.93, 95, 99), Jean Taylor (p.105, 107, 108), Ally Schofield (p.47, 49, 51, 55), Mary Thornton (p.118), John Luffrum (p.138) Jane Moss-Luffrum (p.141, 142, 144, 145,148), all other photos copyright of Philip Hewitson.

First published in the UK in 2024 by Caldew Press.

Caldew Press
12 St George's Crescent
Carlisle
CA3 9NL
www.caldewpress.com

Printed by Lighting Source, UK Ltd.

CALDEW PRESS